LINC

Book Cover by Y'all. That Graphic

Editor- Sandy Ebel, Personal Touch Editing.

Your mental health and emotional well-being matters to me. You can find a list of possible triggers on the book's page on my website or by scanning the QR code below.
Xoxo

CONTENTS

To my husband for being the man I didn't even know I could dream of. Love you, babe.

CHAPTER ONE
LINC

"**F**uck, man, I'm beat to shite," my best friend and partner in crime says across the sticky diner booth in the middle of bumfuck nowhere.

"I can tell. Your fake British accent gets thicker." I take a sip of the coffee in front of me, not bad for a diner, and give Jude a teasing wink.

"Fuck you very much, mate. My accent is one hundred percent approved by the queen herself. You're just upset it lands more birds than that stupid east coast accent you have."

I roll my eyes. Neither of us has any issues in that department. Being members of the Black Roses MC doesn't exactly hurt, either.

"Care to make a wager?"

That piques my interest. "Sure. What did you have in mind?"

Jude's answer is a devious smile as he raises his cup for a refill. The cute waitress who's been waiting on us comes over with the pot.

"Refill?" the pretty blonde asks.

"Thank you, love," Jude starts. "Say, my best mate and I are in town for the night and wondering if there's anything worthwhile we should check out while we're here."

The poor girl looks confused as hell while he tries to lay on his British charm. It's impossible to stop from chuckling at his stupid question. There ain't shit in this town, which anyone can see.

"Don't mind my friend, sweetheart. He doesn't get out much," I say, saving her from having to answer.

She smiles politely and rubs the small scar above her eyebrow. The movement causes the sleeve of her sweater to move past her wrist. That's when I spot the bruises around the small bone. I instantly look at Jude, and he notices the same thing I do.

"Thanks for the coffee, Charlie," I say, reading her name tag. "I'm Linc, and this is my idiot friend, Jude."

She lets out a small giggle. This girl, who can't be more than eighteen or nineteen max, doesn't need to be the prize in a stupid bet with Jude. She needs someone to care about what the fuck happens to her. There's nothing that pisses me off more than seeing a sweet young thing like her being beaten on.

"If you need anything else, let me know. Your food should be up in a minute." Charlie smiles and leaves the table.

As I watch her go, I notice how baggy her uniform is under her too-large sweater. Some women feel more comfortable hiding their curves, while others do it to try to hide themselves entirely. I have a feeling Charlie falls under the second category.

Noticing my irritated scowl, Jude pipes up from across the table.

"Leave it alone, Linc. It's not our business."

He isn't wrong, but that doesn't mean I have to like it or even agree with what he's saying.

"Well, it should be someone's business," I mumble, stretching my neck from side to side.

"I, for one, can't wait to get home and cuddle up with Tiffany," Jude says, changing the subject.

"For some reason, I don't think cuddling is what you have in mind."

Jude and I are making a quick run for the MC. It was nothing big, and we didn't expect any issues, so I took the truck while Jude and a couple of other brothers rode their bikes. The other two we had with us opted to head back to our hometown, Shine, while Jude and I decided to crash for the night. Usually, we would all ride together, but no one saw any signs of trouble, and Jude just had to get his beauty rest. I would've loved to have driven straight through, but there was no way I was going to leave him by himself. Lord only knows what kind of trouble he would find himself in.

When Charlie returns with our food, Jude gives me another warning look. He knows what violence against women means to me. I grew up with a single mother who had a broken picker, as my club's president's mom used to say. After finally leaving Nebraska and my piece-of-shit father behind, we found a home in Shine, Massachusetts. My mom needed a fresh start and liked the snow better there than in Nebraska, whatever that meant. We moved to a small working-class town, where she found a job as a receptionist/office manager for the local bike shop. We were immediately taken into the fold of the Black Roses MC. Janine, the wife of the president at the time, knew from the start that my mom needed someone to give her a shot and a family. That's precisely what we found and haven't looked back.

The life we had before finding Shine and the club became a dim memory. Unfortunately, the scars left behind never seemed to fade. At least not for me.

That's why the only things I involve myself in are bikes and my brothers. Sure, I fuck around with the club bunnies every now and again, a man has needs after all, but I don't ever plan on getting tied down. There's no doubt in my mind I would rather cut off my own hands than ever raise them in anger toward a woman, but there's plenty of damage that can be done that isn't physical. There has never been a time in my life when I thought one woman would be it for me, not even in high school. I'll be damned if I'm ever responsible for breaking some poor girl's heart or vice versa.

As Jude and I are shoveling greasy bacon and some of the best pancakes I've ever tasted in our mouths, the front door of the diner swings open.

A group of loud men walks in, obviously drunk and possibly high on something. From the time my brother and I were young, I developed an almost sixth sense to be able to detect when a situation could go from bad to worse. Considering how we lived for the first several years of our lives, it became second nature and saved our asses on more than one occasion.

Looking at Charlie, I see her trying to figure out which direction this situation is going to land. A tight smile plays on her lips as one of these assholes walks up to her and grabs her in a tight hug. She's like a deer in headlights as her eyes dart between the three men in front of her. I'm about to get up from the booth and teach this asshole some manners, but the slight shake of Jude's head stops me. There are four of them and two of us—not terrible odds, considering Jude's extensive training from the Royal Marines and our experience in taking out trash like this. But seeing as we're the strangers in this town, a night in jail for tearing up a diner isn't a position either of us needs to put ourselves in. Our president, Trick, would have our asses for sure. However, if he lays a hand on her, all bets are off, and Jude will just have to deal with a bench instead of a bed to catch up on his beauty rest.

"Hey, babe," the guy holding Charlie slurs. "How's it been tonight? Looks dead as fuck." He leans down and gives her a disgustingly wet kiss on the mouth before she squirms out of his hold.

"Jace, I'm at work," she says softly, with a nervous smile. Seems Charlie also has a lot of experience in sensing when a situation can go sideways.

Jace rolls his eyes and looks at his three friends, who are watching the scene with glazed indifference.

"Who cares? No one's in here." He gives Jude and me a passing glance but doesn't seem to view us as any sort of threat. This guy obviously doesn't have the self-preservation instincts people like Charlie and I have perfected over the years.

"I just came in to see if you had some cash. Me and the boys were on our way to the store, and I'm a little short on funds."

Memories of my old man coming around to ask for money filter through my head. So do the bruises he left on my mom when she didn't have any to give him.

"Uhh," Charlie stammers. "I have like ten dollars." She fishes around in her pocket, pulling out a five and a few ones from her apron. "Sorry, it's been slow tonight."

When she hands the money over, she tensely waits for his reaction.

The asshole lets out an irritated sigh but grabs the money.

"Fine. Hopefully, it picks up tonight. Or maybe you should try to work more shifts. We aren't going to be able to live off ten dollars a night."

God, what a fucking dick.

"See you after work," Jace tells her before laying another obscene kiss on Charlie's forced smile.

When he passes our table, his eyes meet mine. There is nothing friendly in his gaze, and I'm sure he can see the disgust in mine. I refuse to break his stare because fuck that guy. He's too drunk to realize I'm the apex predator in this place, not him. Guys like him and his low-life friends only pick on people they see as weaker. That's most certainly not me and the 6'3" Englishman sitting across from me.

When they leave, I look at Charlie, wiping his kiss from her mouth. If she was mine, she would never try to wipe the feeling of my lips away.

Woah, where did that thought come from?

Charlie does her best to pull herself together, and before she turns to Jude and me, her mask is firmly back in place. The one women wear when they need to make everyone believe everything is okay and nothing out of the ordinary is going on. I have a feeling she wears that mask regularly.

We finish up our food, and when Charlie brings us the check, I lay a few fifties on the table.

"Um, let me get your change," she says, grabbing the money.

"No change," I tell her.

"That's way too much." She stares at me with those deep blue eyes. "Your bill is only thirty dollars."

"No change," I say again, this time a little more firmly. Damn, since when did I have to start forcing a good tip on a waitress?

Jude and I rise from the booth, and it's the first time Charlie sees me at my full height. She takes in my 6'3" frame, stacked with muscle I got from playing football in high school and still work to keep. Instead of being frightened of someone my size like I would imagine, she swallows and tips her mouth up in a soft smile. This one isn't forced like the one she gave her boyfriend.

"Thank you." She nods once and turns to check on the only other occupied table in the place.

With my good deed done for the night, Jude and I leave the diner, grab a six-pack from the convenience store next to our outdated motel, and head back to our room.

"Damn, Linc. I thought for sure I was going to be helping you cover up a murder by the looks you were giving that girl's old man," Jude says after getting comfortable on his queen-sized mattress.

My jaw clenches as the scene in the diner replays in my mind.

"Don't hulk out on me," he continues, watching my expression through weary eyes. "We just need to get a good night's sleep, then get back to Shine. There's nothing we can do for some girl in a nowhere town. We head out in the morning, and she's still going to be stuck here, living her life."

Jude knows me too well. He can tell I would love nothing more than to find that piece of shit who reminds me too much of my father and beat the shit out of him. Make him pay for his sins and my dad's.

Rising from the bed I was lounging on, I finish my beer. It's the first and only one I'll have tonight. Too many memories plague me of too many nights hiding in my room with my brother while my dad went on a drunken rampage throughout the house. I vowed a long time ago I would never end up like him, drunk and volatile.

"I'm going for a drive," I tell Jude. "I'm too amped up to stay in this shitty room."

"Hey, this is the best... wait, what's the name of this town?"

"Liberty."

"Right. This is the best Liberty has to offer. Don't be such a bougie asshole."

I arch a brow and give Jude an exasperated glare. We've spent way too much time together these last few days.

"Whatever, man. I'll be back in a few."

"Great, more ale for me," he cheers, opening another bottle.

"Don't get so wasted you can't ride tomorrow. I want to get the hell out of here bright and early." The sooner we're away from this town and the trouble I could get myself into, the better.

Grabbing the keys, I make my way to the truck, thinking about the name of this little town—Liberty. Such a sweet name for what seems like a town most people don't escape from. I remember my mom thinking she would never be able to leave that little town in Nebraska.

Me and my brother, Knox, had begged her to leave. Just pack up our meager belongings and get out. For years, my mom always said we couldn't, that we had nowhere to go. Until one day, my dad turned his fists on Knox. That was it for her. He came looking for money, and when she didn't have any to give, he decided to take his anger out on her oldest son, who wasn't his biologically. My tiny frame attacked him from behind, but he threw me off without thought. That's when my mom smacked him in the head with a pan, screaming at him to get out. Though the blow didn't knock him out, it dazed him for a moment.

It was enough time for my mom to grab us and make a run for her room. All we heard was him banging around the house, presumably tearing it apart, looking for the cash he was sure she was always hiding. When we heard the wheels of his beat-to-hell pickup truck screech down the street, my mom didn't waste a second. She threw as much as she could into her small sedan, and we took off, driving through the night, only stopping for gas and ice for my brother's swollen cheek.

I didn't understand at the time why she stopped in Shine, Massachusetts. There was something about being on a river that was constantly moving, always flowing to somewhere else that made her feel safe again. It reminded her if she had to leave, she could follow the river. She would never be stuck again. My mom didn't date again until years later when the friendship she developed with the now president of the Black Roses turned into something more. For a long while, she didn't tell us boys that she had been spending time with Trick outside of the shop. I think she was afraid we would be worried about it ending and us having to leave the only place that ever felt safe for my brother and me. Not like Trick's mom, Janine, would have let that happen. We were family from day one, and nothing was going to change that.

I usually don't let myself think about the sad parts of my past, but there was something about meeting Charlie that brought up those old memories. She reminds me too much of my mom and that time. It's a good thing we're leaving tomorrow. No use getting worked up about some girl in a diner who I don't know and definitely can't help, not in any real way.

Driving for over an hour, I decide I should probably head back to the room to make sure Jude isn't drunk off his ass or hasn't wandered to some seedy bar and brought a girl back to the motel. Unfortunately, it's happened before, and I'm not looking for a repeat. Of course, that's when the skies open up and start pouring rain. These Midwest summer thunderstorms are nothing to fuck around with. I've been stuck in plenty on my bike. At least I'm in the truck.

Just as I'm about to turn around, I see a petite figure walking down the side of the deserted street. Figuring it's either a woman by herself or a kid, and the fact that it's after midnight, I slow down and pull up to the person to make sure everything is okay. That's when I see it's a woman with long blonde hair hanging like a wet curtain around her face, her arms protectively wrapped around her familiar frame. When she looks up, I notice her tear-stained cheek is red and swollen, with a cut above her terrified eyes. When Charlie's gaze meets mine through the glass, she looks seconds from breaking.

I roll down my window. "Do you remember me from the diner?"

"Yeah," she replies in a broken whisper, barely audible above the loud rain drenching her from head to toe.

"Get in." I reach over and open the door from the inside. Charlie grabs the door and winces, clutching her ribs tighter.

When she settles in, I'm seething with rage. Every beating my mom took, every slap and punch I witnessed, is playing like a movie reel through my mind. Every time I watched her clean her cuts and ice her bruises is like another punch to my gut.

We sit in the middle of the road for a few moments while I clutch the steering wheel to keep my fist from flying through the dash. This poor girl doesn't need to be more scared than she already is. I swore to myself I wouldn't get involved, but that was before my suspicions were confirmed.

"I'm guessing this isn't the first time?" Why am I asking? I saw the bruises on her wrist earlier tonight. It's not like I need a full account of every beating. Her palpable fear at the diner and the state I just found her in tells me she's been dealing with this for some time.

Charlie closes her eyes and swallows before a breath escapes through her cut lip.

"No." One word and that asshole's fate is sealed. I know what she's going through, and for whatever reason, she thinks she can't leave. She feels trapped and alone. This is the last night she'll ever feel like that again.

"Where is he?"

CHAPTER TWO
CHARLIE

H e promised he wouldn't do it again. I don't know why I'm surprised he didn't keep his promise this time. When Jace and his friends came to the diner tonight, I saw the look in his eye. I knew that look all too well, though it's been months since I'd seen it. He was high again—another promise he broke. Whenever Jace decides to "party" with his friends, there's more than drinking involved... a lot more. I should stay away tonight. He probably won't notice—maybe—but if he does... I close my eyes as the memory of last time I was late coming home sails through my mind. It's as though I know what's going to happen and just want to get it over with. God, is that what my life has come to? Accepting that the beatings are going to happen and deal with the aftermath? We've been doing this for the last couple of years and every time, he says it won't happen again. When will I stop believing him?

As soon as I walk into the rundown trailer we live in, I know for certain shit's about to go sideways. There are beer bottles littering the large coffee table in front of our couch where three of his friends are sitting.

I put on a brave face and smile, saying polite hellos to the scumbags before going into our bedroom to change out of my dirty work uniform. Looking at myself in the mirror, I debate staying in here for the rest of the night, but last time I did that, Jace accused me of thinking I was too good for everyone.

Put on your big girl panties, Charlie. Maybe it's not as bad as you think.

Throwing on a pair of loose jeans and a long-sleeved baggy t-shirt that covers the bruises on my wrist since Jace doesn't like looking at the evidence of his rough hand, I head into the kitchen.

Damn, I wish I would have brought some food home from the diner. These guys could probably use something to soak up some of the alcohol they've been drinking all night. I search through the fridge but come up empty. Opening the freezer, I find a couple of frozen pizzas.

"Hey, you guys hungry? I'm gonna throw some pizzas in the oven."

"Sure, sounds good," one of the guys replies.

The way Jace is staring at me when his friend answers sets off those familiar warning bells in my mind. He's waiting for any indication he can use to convince himself I'm flirting with them. Like that would ever happen. I hate these guys with a passion. They're not the same friends we had in high school. Most of them moved away after graduation, and the ones who stayed never come around anymore, not that I could blame them.

This new Jace isn't the same likable goofball he was in school. This one is angry and mean. So fucking mean.

Jace's ringing phone sounds through the tiny trailer as I'm putting the pizzas in the oven.

"Yeah," he answers, and listens for a moment to whoever is on the other end. "About time. I'll send Mike and a couple guys to grab it." He hangs up and turns to his friends. "Tre came through. Go grab the shit so we can really get this party going."

His friends heft themselves from the couch and stumble to the door. The second they're out of the trailer, Jace ambles into the kitchen and smacks me across the face.

"I saw the way you were looking at Mike, bitch. How dare you embarrass me like that, panting after my friends?" He grabs me by the hair and yanks my head to his. "They're gonna think I can't keep my woman satisfied."

"No Jace, I swear I wasn't looking at him like that. I just wanted you guys to have something to eat," I cry, my scalp burning from where his hands are yanking at my hair. That earns me another slap, cutting my lip open before he shoves me away. I don't know why I don't just keep my mouth shut. It's not like defending myself when he's like this has ever done any good.

I try to leave the room, to get to my bedroom and to some sort of imaginary safety, but Jace isn't finished. He grabs me by the back of the hair and throws me to the ground, my head smacking against the coffee table when I go down. The entire time, I'm wondering how I'm going to cover the marks he's leaving for my next shift at work. Not how to stop him because I know that's going to be impossible when he's so full of rage, but how am I going to pull off looking like my life isn't the horror show it's turned into?

I'm begging him to stop as blood pours into my eye, tingeing everything a murky red. A sharp kick to the ribs has me curling in on myself, trying to prevent any more damage. It's terrifying not looking at him when he's raging like this, not being able to see what he's going to do next, but I know sometimes catching his eye sets him off even more. I'm not sure if it's because he hates himself for the fear he sees in my gaze or if he takes it as a challenge, probably the latter. Either way, there are times it makes the beatings worse, so I don't dare look at him now. I feel him standing over me, breathing heavy but not moving. After a few moments, he lets out a sound of disgust and moves to the kitchen.

"I don't know why you make me do this. Maybe one of these days you'll learn." He walks back into the living room, stepping over my balled-up form like I'm just a pile of dirty laundry he doesn't want to deal with. "Get up and go get cleaned up. You're a fucking mess," he sneers, opening another bottle and sitting on his ratty recliner.

I gingerly stand up from the dirt-stained floor, minding my bruised ribs, and make my way to the bedroom. In my little bathroom, I check myself in the mirror. The cut on my lip has stopped bleeding, but the wound on my forehead is still oozing. Grabbing some bandages from under the sink, I attempt to cover my eyebrow, but within a minute, the blood seeps through. I take the bandage off, throw it in the sink, and stare at my reflection. I'm going to die here. Maybe not tonight, but there is no doubt in my mind this will be my life until my last breath if I don't find a way out.

While staring at my hollow eyes in the mirror, I hear the door to the trailer bang open. Jace's friends are back. One of them tells him they scored some "good shit."

Good for who?

When music starts blaring from the living room, I hear the telltale signs of them snorting whatever it is they showed up with. I know if I didn't get out now, I'm dead. It won't be long before Jace kills me. He doesn't even pretend to care anymore about the damage he does to the person he's supposed to love. That was made more than apparent tonight. Shit, it's been more than apparent for more than a year. I have a choice to make. I can stay until he's sober enough to have a conversation, or I can run. Tonight. Right now.

Without thinking about anything other than getting the hell out, I quietly open the window in our bedroom. There's no way I can grab the cash I have stashed away in the laundry room Jace never visits. The day he washes his own clothes is the day I win the damn lottery. That's women's work, he's always told me. All I have is the money from the tip Linc left me and a few extra dollars in the pocket of my uniform, which I haven't thrown in the wash yet.

I can walk to the rundown motel on the other side of town and come up with a plan. If I leave now, I'll be there before Jace thinks to come look for me tonight. They'll be up snorting lines and drinking for hours.

It's a small jump from the window. When I land, the pain in my abused ribs from the jolt nearly makes me cry out, but I suck it up like I have so many other times. Running out of the trailer park, I sprint from shadow to shadow, knowing there will be no sense of safety until I make it to the motel. Hell, probably not even then. I can't think of that now. I just need to get as far away as quickly as I can.

A sigh of relief escapes me as soon as the lights from the entrance of the trailer park are no longer visible every time I look behind me. He hasn't figured out I'm gone yet. Otherwise, he would already be dragging me back to the trailer, high or not.

After half an hour of walking, the rain starts coming down hard. My clothes are stuck to me, and my shoes are soaked through, but I keep walking. No cars pass, not that there is ever much activity on this stretch of road late at night. That brings me some relief. The only people who would be driving down here would be someone who lives in the trailer park. Jace and I know most everyone there, and I doubt it would take long for someone to go knocking and ask him why they saw me on the side of the road in a rainstorm.

That relief is short-lived when I see headlights approaching through the curtain of rain pouring down. Anxiety fills me, but I keep my head down, praying if it's someone from the park, they won't recognize me.

The truck slows, and I briefly consider running into the woods and hiding, hoping they'll pass without stopping. I don't have any sort of flashlight, so all it would take is one wrong move, and I'd break my ankle and be stuck there.

The truck slowly rolls past, and I think I'm in the clear until the diver turns the truck around. When I hear the rumbling engine pull up next to me, they roll down the window. I chance a glance at them and immediately recognize the man's face from earlier. Linc.

"Do you remember me from the diner?"

I nod, barely able to look him in the eye. I know he saw the bruises on my wrist from a week ago. That time, it was because I was making too much noise cleaning when Jace was trying to sleep. He decided to stop me by nearly breaking the bone.

"Get in," he says, opening the door from the inside.

I pause because, although he and his friend seemed nice enough at the diner, he's still a stranger. Not that he could be any more of a monster than the one I just left in that dingy trailer.

When our gazes meet, I see him cataloging every visible injury. He now knows the bruises he saw on my wrist earlier couldn't be from anything other than what they were, what I'm sure he suspected. Shame overwhelms me—complete and utter shame. He's probably wondering why I stayed with a man who beats on women, or worse, what I did to deserve this. There's no time to worry about what some stranger thinks of me. Not when Jace could come looking for me any minute. That fear is enough to make my decision for me.

I get in the truck, trying to hide the pain in my ribs, but he catches the way I hug them just a little tighter. His hands grip the steering wheel, causing his knuckles to turn white.

"I'm guessing this isn't the first time?"

"No." I shake my head. Though this isn't the first time Jace has hit me, this is the first time I've admitted to anyone what goes on behind closed doors.

"Where is he?" Linc growls.

The question startles me. "Why?"

Linc's gaze bores into mine, and the storm I see brewing in his eyes promises violence and retribution. I should be scared. I'm in the company of a violent man. He doesn't try to hide it, and I can read his face clear as day. I've gotten quite adept at reading someone's body language. With Linc, though, it's not the same expression I've seen so many other times in Jace's eyes. His anger isn't directed *at* me but what's been done *to* me.

"Because no man has the right to put his hands on a woman. Ever."

I nod, acknowledging what he said, but I'm still confused. Why would a stranger I just met tonight want to get mixed up in this mess? Jace is dangerous. He's erratic and unpredictable, not to mention connected to a criminal organization, but he doesn't know that I know that.

"Were you leaving him?"

"Yeah." The word comes out in a broken whisper, so quiet to my own ears compared to the storm raging outside the truck. I squeeze my eyes shut as shame washes over me again. Why did it take me so long to make this decision?

"You don't have anything with you?"

"There was no time." I didn't even grab my phone, which is still in the kitchen. God, I am so freaking stupid.

Linc lets out a slow breath and fixes me with his stare.

"Let's go get your stuff, then."

He turns the truck around, and we head back in the direction I was walking from.

"I can't just go back in there," I say in a small voice. "He won't let me leave again."

And it will be even worse if I go back.

"He'll let you, Charlie. I'll make sure of it." He sounds so sure, as if it's going to be that easy.

"Jace is dangerous. He has a couple friends there, too. I don't think this is the best idea." None of this was a good idea. I should have waited, prepared.

A dark chuckle escapes Linc. "He has no idea what a dangerous man looks like."

With nothing to say to that and no fight left in me, I give him directions to the trailer park. When we pull up, I spot his friend's car still parked in front.

"There're three guys in there with him." My warning seems to fall on deaf ears as he stares at the trailer. A war is raging inside of Linc. I can feel it. I don't know who it's with, or who is going to win.

"We don't have to do this," I try one more time. "I can come back when he isn't around." Though he rarely leaves these days, and he'll more than likely be here waiting for me if he thinks I'll come back for my things. That doesn't mean I want to watch someone get hurt trying to help me now, though.

There's more than just his temper that makes Jace dangerous. Linc needs to know what he's getting himself into. Just as I'm about to explain, Linc reaches under his seat and pulls out a gun. He checks the clip and I'm stunned that he's driving around with a loaded weapon.

Who is this man?

Linc turns to me while my mind is racing, thinking of all the possibilities of why he's holding a gun. He gently sweeps his hand just above the cut on my forehead, then down to my split lip. The pain I see in his eyes doesn't seem to be for me. It's almost as though he's seeing someone else.

"Wait in the truck. I'll come get you when it's safe."

Linc gets out and walks to the flimsy door, kicking it in. I jump in my seat and open the passenger door when Jace's friends tumble out of the trailer, making a run for it. They get in their car and peel away, throwing up gravel in their wake. I rush away from the truck and run to the busted door. Inside, Linc has his gun raised, and it's pointed at Jace.

"Make a move, motherfucker. Give me a reason."

Jace's glare meets my wide eyes, and the movement distracts Linc for a moment. He looks back at me while his gun is still on Jace, but the momentary shift in his focus is enough to give Jace the chance to rush Linc. I watch in horror as both men fall to the floor. The gun slips from Linc's grip before he flips them over and Linc lands on top, raining blow after blow to Jace's face. I'm frozen solid as I watch Linc become completely un-hinged. I don't even recognize Jace's face after what can only be mere moments. The sound of his bones crunch-ing under Linc's punishing blows echoes through the tiny trailer. Jace isn't moving or fighting back, but that doesn't stop Linc. I'm not sure he realizes that Jace is no longer conscious.

I break myself out of my frozen stupor and run over to them.

"Linc, stop. Please," I beg. I'm not begging for Jace, but I don't want Linc to be arrested on murder charges, and by the way he's so brutally beating Jace, it's a very real possibility Jace won't live to see tomorrow.

"Please," I cry again and lay my hand on his back. Probably not the smartest move, considering I don't think Linc is fully aware at the moment, but somehow, I know he won't hurt me.

My touch jolts him out of the haze of violence he seems trapped in.

Linc looks from me to the bloody body under him, then back to me. He stands and my hand grazes his face. His eyes close for a moment, and when he opens them, I can tell he's back and fully present again.

"Go get your stuff," he says in a hoarse whisper.

I run to my room and grab a bag, hurriedly opening dresser drawers and shoving clothes inside. Then I rush out of the bedroom into the laundry room, where I have my meager stash of cash hidden in an old detergent box on the top shelf of the cabinet.

When I reach the living room, Jace still hasn't moved from the floor. I can't tell if he's passed out or if his eyes are so swollen, he can't open them.

"Is he dead?" I ask Linc.

"No, the piece of shit will live to see another day, but we need to get out of here." The gun is in Linc's hand once again while he waits for me by the door, keeping it trained on Jace.

Closing my eyes, I take a steadying breath. I never thought I would get out of here in one piece, or at all, for that matter. Relief washes over me when my eyes open and look around the room. My gaze catches on a book that Jace always kept close. I've heard him talking about what's inside. On a whim, I grab the notebook and shove it in my bag.

"Let's go," I tell Linc as we make our way back to his truck.

I have no idea where life will take me now. I'm leaving the only place, the only town, I've ever called home. I'm scared to fucking death about my future, but I'm free.

Linc jumps in the truck and turns to me.

"Where to?"

Isn't that the million-dollar question?

"I have no idea."

Linc nods and starts the truck.

"How about you come back to the hotel, and we'll figure it out from there?"

"I've never been on my own," I tell him in a shaky voice, so scared he'll just drop me off and expect me to know what to do.

"Well," he begins as he backs away from the trailer. "It's a good thing you have me, then. We'll get you sorted, Charlie. I won't leave you until you're safe."

Safe. That certainly isn't a word that could have ever been used to describe my life.

We're almost to the exit of the trailer park when three police cars turn in from the road and stop in front of us with their sirens blaring and lights flashing.

"Get out of the truck with your hands in the air," one of the officers calls from a microphone.

My terrified gaze turns to Linc, and the pain in his eyes makes mine well up with tears.

"Linc?" I don't know what I'm asking or what I want him to tell me. It's not like he can reassure me. He just beat the hell out of Jace, not to mention the gun stowed under his seat.

"Don't say anything. You weren't in the trailer. Understand?"

I nod as a lone tear escapes.

Linc rests a hand on my cheek, his stare boring into me.

"I don't regret it, Charlie. Not a damn thing."

Linc reaches over and opens his truck door, slowly exiting the vehicle with his hand in the air.

I know right then and there that in trying to give me my freedom, Linc just lost his.

Chapter Three
Linc
Six Years Later

I t's been months of nonstop partying with a different woman in my bed, or out of it, depending on the mood I'm in. After being released from prison, I was getting back to my real life. Fuck, being locked away for six years was fucking brutal. Will I ever regret what I got sent away for? No. To this day I still don't. But it would have been nice if Charlie had stuck around and testified on my behalf. Thank God the club has a top-notch attorney, but I could have probably had my sentence reduced for extenuating circumstances had she been at the courthouse.

Our new president, Ozzy, tried to find her, but that girl was in the wind. I'm not particularly bitter about it, not like some of my other brothers, especially Jude. He couldn't comprehend why someone whose life I'd saved bailed on me. He fails to understand, after what that fuckhead put her through, she'd been terrified of never getting away. There was a desperation I saw in her that he hadn't. I'll never blame her for that.

I got out after six years of a ten-year sentence for good behavior and overcrowding. Fortunately, good behavior only counts in prison because since I've been out, my behavior has been anything but.

Speaking of bad behavior, I turn to find my latest late night bad decision next to me. I usually don't let the bunnies stay the night in my bed. Once I'm ready to pass out, there's no waking me, therefore no reason for them to be here. Since coming back, I sleep like a fucking baby. Most guys are the opposite, but I hardly slept a wink for six years, so I'm catching up.

"Sweetheart," I tell the sleeping girl in my bed. "You have to get up and go." I'm not trying to be a dick, but I got shit to do today. Prez decided the celebration had lasted long enough, and it's time to get down to business. We're going on a run later today, and we need to finalize everything before we can take off.

"Stacia, honey, come on, up and at 'em."

She groans into the pillow and reaches for me with her hand going straight to my cock. Letting out a soft moan, her hand rubs over the bulge in my boxer briefs.

"Up and at 'em sounds like a plan to me," she says in her most seductive voice.

A chuckle escapes me, and I grab her hand kissing the back of it. Never let it be said I'm not a gentleman.

"Not this morning, sweetheart. I have business to attend to."

She gives me a little pout then rolls over and sits up. Watching her bare tits bounce as she pulls up her tiny shorts has me rethinking my time crunch. I probably have ten minutes to spare... The loud bang on my door shakes me out of my wayward thoughts.

"Let's go, asshole. Put away your tiny prick and get to church." Jude is just as much of a cockblock today as he was six years ago.

"Fuck off," I call back and rise from the bed.

Casting one more look in Stacia's direction, I appreciate the black lace bra that barely contains her perky tits.

"See you when you get back," she sings before blowing me a kiss and heading out the door.

As much as I wouldn't mind having the afternoon to fuck around with her, I'm looking forward to going on a long run. After being locked up for so long, I've taken my bike out nearly every day. Not a day went by in lock-up that I didn't miss the sound of the engine roaring down the open road. Being home and reuniting with my brothers has been everything I knew it would be, but when I got on my bike for the first time, my soul felt at peace. I may have even shed a tear, but no one talks about that.

Church is full by the time I stroll in. I take my seat next to my brother, Knox, The MC's vice president. He looks me over and quirks his lip.

"You have a little something right there," He points to the spot just behind his own ear, and I wipe at mine. My finger comes away with hot pink lipstick smeared across the tip. I give him a wry grin and shrug. My brother chuckles as Ozzy slams the gavel to start the meeting.

A few things have changed since I went away, namely Ozzy, Trick's son, is the new president. When Trick's arthritis got so bad he couldn't grip his handlebars anymore, he decided it was time to retire. Now he and my mom are living it up and happy as pigs in shit. I'm sure she sleeps a little better at night, knowing at least one of the men in her life is safe. Not that she would ever say it out loud. My mom loves this club and everything it's done for our family.

"Alright. The route has been set up for the run today," Ozzy starts. "The Irish have a crew who will meet you in Texas, and they'll be responsible for getting the shit over the border. Four days to get there and four back. Obviously, we aren't expecting any trouble, and I don't want you guys pushing it. This is one of the biggest runs we've done for them. Let's ride under the radar. Linc, Jude and Wyatt, you three will take your bikes. Barrett, you're in the van."

"A road captain in a van." Barrett lets out an irritated sigh. "What is the world coming to?"

Ozzy gives him a look that tells him to shut the hell up. He isn't the sort of prez not to hear his guys out, but when he's giving orders right before a run, he's not about to change his game plan for any grumbling asshole.

"Boys, make sure everyone has the coordinates and the route locked in their phones. You roll out in an hour."

Ozzy slams the gavel, ending church, and everyone in the room stands to leave.

"How you feel about going on a run?" my brother asks when we're the only two left in the room.

"Great. Can't wait for the long days on my bike and hopefully long nights in some pretty young thing's bed." I shoot him a carefree smirk.

I'm not shocked Knox is asking me if I'm good to ride. I'm surprised he waited until now, to be honest.

He gives me a pointed look. "Maybe stay away from any pretty young things on this trip." And there it is—the warning I've been waiting for.

"No worries, brother." I clasp his shoulder and confidently meet his gaze. "There won't be any repeats of last time."

Knox was the one who kept our mom sane while I was gone. Well, her and Trick. They held her up when she wanted to crumble every time she got home from a prison visit. I'll forever be grateful to them, but I have to get on with it now that I'm out. This life will always be dangerous, and there's always a chance any of us could end up doing time. Nothing is going to change that, and my mom knows it.

"Just go say bye to Mom before you leave," Knox tells me and walks out the door. Well there goes my plan for the sendoff I was hoping to get from one of the bunnies.

It's been a grueling three-and-a-half days getting to Texas. We met with the Irish and dropped the guns with them. They get to figure out how to get them across the border. Thank God because that's a headache I don't want to deal with. We're at yet another cheap motel for the night. My ass hurts, I'm hungry, and in need of a beer or seventeen. Now that the guns are gone, we can relax and have a night to let loose before we hit the road tomorrow and get the hell home. Three days riding through back roads, staying on high alert and only stopping for gas station sandwiches, got real old real quick.

"I asked the lady at the counter where to get a good meal, and she said the diner across the way has a decent meatloaf," Wyatt tells us as he comes out of the office of the motel, handing us our keys. "They don't serve alcohol, but there's that little bar we passed on our way in. Let's get cleaned up, get some hot food, then go get some beers."

We all grunt in agreement, and I grab the key. When I get inside, my eyes travel around the old room. It's like every other fleabag motel we've stayed in on this run. Turning on the TV, I'm thankful it works. I toss my bag on the bed and head to the shower. Cranking the water all the way to hot, it's a pleasant surprise to see steam rising almost immediately. A hot shower is just what I need to relax my sore-as-fuck muscles. After drying off and throwing on some clean jeans, I go to the room next door and knock on the door. Jude answers in a towel with his phone in his hand.

"I'll be ready in a sec. Just checking in with my brother."

Jude's brother served in the Royal Marines, same as Jude, but he got out first and moved to the States. He does some under-the-radar shit that's just as dangerous, if not more so, than what Jude and I do. According to him, though, he stays on the right side of the law. I have my doubts.

When he's dressed, we meet the other two guys and head across the street to the diner.

"Damn, Linc, you're walking like you have a stick shoved up your asshole. You okay over there?" Barrett teases.

"Fuck you, asshole. I haven't been on a run in six years. I'm just a little rusty."

"Need to make a switch? You can drive the van, and I'll take your bike back to Shine."

"Not on your life," I volley back.

Barrett is still bitter he had to drive the van instead of ride, but there's no way in hell I'm going to be stuck in a cage.

The older waitress comes to take our order, and Jude gives me a nudge.

"No cute waitresses this time around. Lucky us, huh?"

I give him a side eye and let out an annoyed sigh.

"Got something you want to say about Charlie?" We haven't had this conversation outright. It's mostly been him making comments under his breath about getting stuck in prison because of some bird.

"Yeah, actually I do," Jude snarks. "She took six years of your life, and she's still getting to you. Don't think I don't see the way you've been since you got back."

"What are you talking about?" There's no way he can miss the irritation in my voice. Unfortunately, it doesn't stop him from continuing.

"The way you've been fucking your way through the bunnies and any other girl that comes into the club-house. That was never like you before. Then there's the fact you only go for the ones with blonde hair and blue eyes. The ones that look surprisingly similar to the girl you rescued, who then bailed on you." He takes a sip of his coffee and continues. "Look, I just want to make sure your head's on right. I'm hoping this ride gives you some perspective."

Since when did bikers look down at copious amounts of sex with random women?

"You guys in on this?" I look at Wyatt and Barrett, sitting across from me.

"Not so much in on it as we're concerned, too. The whole club is," Wyatt answers.

I scrape my hand over the four-day stubble I've grown since being on this run.

"Listen, I appreciate the concern, but I'm fine. I haven't heard from Charlie in years. As far as I know, she's moved on with her life, and she's happy. I'm not fucking my way through all the blondes I can find in some attempt to fuck her out of my system. I haven't been all that particular about where I stick my dick the last six months. Same as you assholes." At least, I don't think I have. Never mind that every time I closed my eyes in prison, bright blue eyes stared back at me. Every. Damn. Night. But I haven't tried to find her since coming home. She found a way out of a violent life. I'm not about to drag her or anyone else into one.

Jude whips his head toward me. "What do you mean you heard from her? She was in the wind six years ago."

I may have "forgotten" to mention to my best friend that she wrote to me while I was in prison. His feelings toward the broken girl I found on the side of the road is the reason I kept it to myself.

"When I was inside, she sent me a letter and told me how sorry she was for leaving. Said I saved her life, and she would always be grateful." I shrug like it's no big deal, but I know Jude isn't finished.

Jude's eye twitches and the other two guys' eyes ping-pong between us.

"Jude, you don't understand what it was like for her. She needed to escape, and I gave her that. If she had stayed, I can fucking guarantee that piece of shit would have found her and finished what he started. She had no one, and I was locked up."

"I would have helped her," he says a little too loudly, startling the waitress setting the food on our table.

"Uh...you boys need anything else?" the woman nervously asks, darting her gaze between Jude and me.

"No thank you, ma'am," Barrett answers for us, turning on his Southern charm. No need to scare the woman trying to do her job.

"She didn't know that, Jude," I say in a quieter voice. "She was scared and lost. She apologized for leaving in the letter, but she was running for her life. Who's to say her testimony would have helped, anyway? They found the gun, and I beat that fucker half to death. And you want to know something else?" I ask before taking a bite of the best damn meatloaf I've had outside of my mom's. "I would have done it again, even knowing I'd spend time in prison. I would have done it all again." I chew the meatloaf and moan in pleasure.

Jude is watching me like I've lost my damn mind.

"So what? You plan on finding her? Making her your old lady now that you're out? Has fucking every girl who looks like her just been a coincidence? Or are you just sowing some wild oats?"

"Jesus fucking Christ. Can a man eat in fucking peace without you throwing twenty questions at him?" I take a bite of my meatloaf and glare at him while I finish chewing and swallow. "No, I don't plan on finding her. I never wrote her back. She was happy living in New Orleans. That's all I need to know."

What I don't tell him is the way her eyes haunted me when I was inside. Not the terrified eyes of the girl I picked up in the rain, but when she smiled at me in the diner. It was as though she didn't believe there were kind souls in the world willing to help a girl who so desperately needed it. I don't tell him the number of times I read her letter and imagined her happy and smiling in her new life. I never got to see that, but damn, I wish I had.

"Well, at least you saw reason. Linc, this girl didn't come to your defense. She basically let you rot in jail."

Jude is right in a way. She did leave me to fight the charges on my own, but here's the thing—she'd been fighting on her own the entire time she was being beaten by her boyfriend. She saw an opportunity to get away from the hell she was living in. I'll never hold that against her. I was a big boy and knew exactly what was going to happen the second I saw those flashing lights. I hadn't wanted her to stick around. I'd done plenty of things to land me in jail. That was just the one thing I got caught for.

"Doesn't matter. She's living in New Orleans, and I'm not. But understand this Jude, I don't hold anything against her, and neither should you. Heaven help you if you ever find yourself in the situation I was faced with. I doubt you would have made a different decision."

"Don't count on it, mate," Jude scoffs. "I like my freedom way too much to get tangled up in that kind of mess."

"Can we please drop it? I'd like to eat my meatloaf in peace and have a few beers with my brothers. No use crying about something done and over with. I'm out, and I'll never see her again. End of."

Jude nods, hopefully dropping the subject to never bring it up again.

After finishing our dinner, we decide to grab the van from the hotel parking lot and head to the bar that's about a mile down the road. Our bikes would likely draw too much attention in this sleepy town at this time of night. The last thing we need is some drunk locals deciding they don't want a bunch of bikers around. We learned the hard way years ago that Texas can be tricky like that. We aren't the sort of club that has brothers with something to prove. There's only four of us here, and since my stint in jail, everyone has taken to keeping a low profile on runs. No need to cause a stir when we don't have to.

We pull up to the bar that's nothing more than a nondescript brick building on the edge of town. The only indication they serve alcohol is the few neon beer signs hanging in the blacked-out windows and the sign above the door.

"Jimmy John's Bar," Wyatt mutters. "Real original."

Barret opens the door to a low-lit open space, with the bar on one side of the room, tables in the middle, and pool tables on the other side. Your typical blue-collar watering hole, and just the kind of place we all feel most at home.

"Nice, they have darts," Jude comments when he spots the well-used dart boards hanging on the back wall.

Barrett shakes his head. "What is it with you and darts?"

"That shit was his national pastime in England. He's been playing since he was old enough to throw straight," Wyatt replies.

"Too true, mate. Anyone care to make a wager?"

We all groan. No one in the club has ever been able to beat him in a game.

"Spoil sports," Liam whines as he and Wyatt grab a table.

There aren't many people here at this hour, which doesn't surprise me. It's not too late, but it strikes me as the kind of town where the regulars wake up early for work and aren't out late drinking on a Tuesday night.

The waitress walks over to the only other customers in the place, playing pool with a tray of beers. "I'll be right with you," she calls as she hands the men their drinks.

Barrett and I belly up to the bar and scope out their whiskey selection.

"Char, you have some customers," the raven-haired waitress shouts.

"Coming," I hear a voice calling from the back. The bartender comes through the swinging doors with a case of beer and hauls it onto the counter next to the cooler, blowing an errant hair off her face with a huff.

"What can I get for you?" she asks before looking up.

When she does, my gaze collides with bright blue eyes I haven't seen in over six years. *Holy shit.*

"Charlie?"

CHAPTER FOUR
CHARLIE

N o way. *No fucking way.* Linc is sitting in my bar in bumfuck nowhere Texas. And he recognized me.

The last time we saw each other, I was six years younger, too skinny for my 5'6" frame, blonde, and beaten to hell. Since that night all those years ago, I've gained about twenty pounds and started dying my hair dark brown. I thought I looked different enough that no one would recognize me.

Apparently not.

God, he looks just like he did six years ago. His brown hair is a little longer, and he didn't have the almost beard back then, but those eyes. They're the same hazel ones that promised me everything would be okay all those years ago. The ones that, had we met at a different time and under different circumstances, I could have lost myself in. You know, the typical way a teenage girl fantasizes about her dream man. Only difference is I got my dream man sent to prison. I thought about Linc throughout the years, and every time I did, a wave of guilt would nearly drown me. He did so much for me that night and ultimately paid with his freedom.

The fact he's suddenly sitting at my bar is too much of a coincidence not to be suspicious, though. Does he know what I took from Jace the night he was arrested? The only people who could know how valuable the notebook I stole was Jace, me, the people he seriously screwed over by keeping that information, and the people who would probably like to get their hands on it. There was no doubt in my mind the last two groups had no idea he had it. At least, they didn't six years ago.

"What are you doing here?" I ask, too stunned to think of anything more clever. "Why are you here?"

"Why aren't you in New Orleans?" he asks, looking just as surprised as I feel.

The guy sitting next to him watches as we stare at each other, tossing questions back and forth, without either of us answering the other's.

"Shit, Charlie." Linc shakes his head and lets out a low whistle. "I thought you were in a completely different city living a happy life. How the hell did you end up in this shithole?"

My neck bristles with irritation for the town my best friend Lucy and I decided to call home for the foreseeable future. I don't know why, we've only been here for a few months, but the people here welcomed us without asking a million questions neither of us had answers for. If he thought this was a shithole, he obviously wasn't paying attention to where he found me that night over six years ago.

"This is Charlie?" the guy sitting next to Linc chimes in. "Guess you were wasting your time fucking all those blondes." He chuckles, and Linc shoots him an irritated scowl.

"Shut up, Wyatt," he says through gritted teeth.

"New Orleans didn't work out. I needed a fresh start, and this place seemed as good as any."

Everything was going fine for the first couple years I lived there. I'd finally made some friends and had an apartment with a roommate, Lucy, who became more like a sister to me than a roommate. I had a job I liked working in a bar, where I first met Lucy. I was happy. Free. New Orleans was supposed to be far enough away and busy enough that no one would be able to find me there. A needle in a haystack, as they say. It all came crashing down the day I spotted Jace's cousin walking across the street from the bar where I was waitressing. I don't know how he found me in New Orleans, but considering what I had on his organization, I wasn't about to walk up to him and ask.

I rushed back to the little apartment Lucy and I shared and started packing. She was scheduled to work later that night, but when she saw the look of terror in my eyes, she didn't ask any questions and began throwing her things in a bag next to me. When I tried to argue with her about running with me, she told me there was no way she was letting me leave without her. Lucy made it clear that family stuck together, and she was mine.

"Hey, Linc, stop flirting with the bartender and grab us some beers, would ya?" a deep voice laced in a familiar British accent calls from one of the tables. When Linc turns toward the side, Jude catches sight of me. "Fuck," he mutters looking toward the ceiling.

The man sitting next to him has no idea why Jude's annoyed as his gaze swings between the two of us.

"She one of the broken hearts you left throughout the continental U.S.?" His laughter dies when he realizes no one else is laughing with him. "What's going on?" he asks, clearly confused with the situation.

Join the club, pal.

"That's Charlie," Jude replies.

A low whistle sounds through the man's teeth. "Well, shit, I don't think beer is going to be enough for this reunion."

The expressions on the faces of the two men at the table are anything but warm. Jude looks at me like I've kicked a puppy or was responsible for his friend losing six years of his life, and the other looks at me with suspicious interest.

Lucy comes behind the bar, putting a comforting hand on my back.

"You okay, sis?"

I've told Lucy all about Linc and my ex, even confiding in her about the notebook I stole and its contents. She's been a little more tight-lipped about her past, only saying she left a bad situation, and she doesn't like to talk about it. Why invite the demons? I can relate, so I never pushed her.

"Are you fucking serious lady?" Jude calls, getting up from the table and coming to stand next to Linc. "She's not the one who spent the last six years in prison."

"Shut up, Jude." Linc gives me an apologetic look.

"I will not," he says, turning toward me. "Where've you been, Charlie? Linc went to prison for taking out your trash, and you let him sit there without ever showing up for the trial or testifying on his behalf. You just took off, so it was your ex's word against his. Did you know they had your statement to the police thrown out because they couldn't find you? Jace's lawyer twisted it to make it sound like Linc was a jealous lover."

"Back off, asshole," Lucy says from next to me. "She doesn't need you throwing shit in her face. You weren't there. You don't know what she was going through. Who the fuck do you think you are to judge her?"

Jude's icy green gaze turns to my best friend, and the arctic look he gives her chills me to the bone.

"Lucy, it's okay. I'll handle it." I'd gotten used to handling men with short fuses in my life. No need to drag Lucy in.

"No, fuck that, Charlie. And fuck this guy for thinking he gets to talk to you like that." She turns and stares Jude in the eye. "Try again, asshole. This time with someone your own size."

It's almost comical considering how tiny Lucy is, but that doesn't stop her from squaring up to a man almost twice her size. Jude may be bigger in stature, but I've never met any man with balls as big as Lucy's. This isn't the first time I've thought if I had someone in my life like her all those years ago, things would have turned out very differently.

Linc stands and puts his hand on Jude's chest, pushing him back a step. That's when I take in what he's wearing. His jacket has a patch on the back that reads the Black Roses MC, Massachusetts. He wasn't wearing it the night we met.

"You're in a motorcycle club," I blurt out.

Linc whirls around, meeting my frightened gaze. I'm not stupid. I know what goes on with motorcycle clubs. They're criminals.

"Yeah, he is, sweetheart, and you're responsible for my brother going to prison," Jude replies caustically.

I'm fucked.

I sent the member of an MC to prison. Even though it wasn't because of anything I did, Jude obviously holds me responsible. Honestly, there were a lot of nights in the last six years I held myself responsible, too. In those first few months, sleep didn't come easy.

The case never made national headlines or anything like that. Rarely do saviors of beaten women get the thanks they deserve. I knew enough details, like the arrest date and the "victim" of the case, so I was able to scour our local paper online to follow the hearing. In a town as small as Liberty, it was a big deal back then, but the paper never mentioned anything about him being involved with an MC. I was still too terrified to go back, though. Never in a million years did I think Linc would get sentenced to ten years. Not after I gave my statement to the police and told them what Jace did to me, even though the damage was stamped across my face. The police were given every detail surrounding my abuse from the last year, including that night.

When he was sent to prison, I sent Linc a letter to tell him how sorry, yet how thankful I was for everything. I never expected him to write back, not that his response would have found me. I spent a lot of time moving from town to town, making my way south. Diners or bars in little nowhere towns didn't care that I didn't have an ID, and I certainly wasn't about to give them my resume. It would have only been a matter of time before word got back to Jace that prospective employers were calling about me.

"I was in an MC back then, too, Charlie, but it's nothing for you to worry about. No matter what Jude says." Linc's mouth forms a tight line as he shoots his friend a warning stare that can't be mistaken for anything other than a threat.

"Yeah, like she's going to believe that." Next to me, Lucy lets out a huff of disgust. "I know all about guys like you and clubs like yours." Considering Lucy hasn't said too much about her past, I wonder how she knows about clubs like Linc's.

"You don't know shit, Lucifer," Jude spits at Lucy.

"Oh, we're at the nickname stage in our relationship? Because I have some really good—"

I cut her off by pulling her back and stepping in front of her. I don't care what Linc says, the look on Jude's face as Lucy lays into him is setting familiar alarms whirling through my head.

The truth of the matter is, although I trusted Linc six years ago, a lot can change. I don't know him, not really. Add in the fact he's in a motorcycle club and probably doesn't always walk on the right side of the law means I'm not taking chances with Lucy.

Linc looks at me with concern swirling in his eyes.

"Jude, you need to back off," he tells the angry man, who is still shooting daggers at my best friend. "I mean it," he reiterates when Jude doesn't make a move to stand down.

"Whatever," Jude finally concedes and goes to sit with one of the other guys he came in with.

Linc turns to the other man sitting next to him. "Wyatt, can we have a minute?"

Wyatt looks between Linc and me and nods. "Sure thing," he replies and stands. "Can I grab a couple of beers first?"

Linc looks ready to tell him to get the hell out of here before Lucy comes from behind me and grabs three beers, plopping them down in front of him.

"There. Now, fuck off," Lucy growls.

Wyatt grabs the beers and nods his head at Linc. "Good luck, brother," he says under his breath. Lucy stares at him as though she could set him on fire with the power of her mind while he walks to the table where his friends are sitting. Wow, she really does not like bikers.

"Can I have a moment with Charlie?" Linc asks Lucy in a soft tone.

She lets out an incredulous laugh. "Not on your life, biker boy," she replies, looking him dead in the eye.

A long sigh escapes an obviously exhausted Linc. I don't know if it's the tense situation or whatever reason they're in Texas, but Linc looks ready to drop.

"Charlie," he starts but gives a slight shake of his head as if he doesn't know what to say. "Listen, don't mind Jude. It's been a long few days, and he can get a bit... prickly after not getting enough sleep."

Lucy scoffs, still standing sentry by my side.

"I'm just a little surprised to see you in Texas is all." Or a lot surprised. "And I didn't know you were in an MC."

"We didn't get much of a chance to talk that night."

No, we certainly did not. I don't know when we would have between him picking me up on the side of the road, then beating the shit out of my ex and getting arrested.

"I like the hair," he tells me, pointing at my dark brown locks. Last time I saw Linc, I was a blonde.

"Yeah, I needed a change." And I needed to change my appearance as quickly as possible. A bottle of hair dye seemed to do the trick; at least, I thought it did. I've gained a few pounds in the last few years, too. It helps that I wasn't constantly anxious about what I was going to find when I got home or what imagined slight I had committed against Jace. I even started wearing makeup. That was something Jace never let me do. He would ask me who I was getting dressed up for if I left the house with it on. The only makeup allowed was concealer to cover up what he did to me when he was in a mood.

Lucy stands next to me at the bar, washing glasses that are already clean in the little sink. She's not at all stealthy in the way she's looking between Linc and me as she listens to the stilted-as-hell conversation we're having.

"So, what are you boys doing in Texas," Lucy asks, taking pity on me and my complete lack of ability to carry a conversation at the moment.

"Club business," Linc replies, glancing at Lucy, then back to me.

"That's pretty vague," I say, wondering if he's going to elaborate.

He doesn't.

"Charlie—"

"Linc—"

We both start at the same time. A nervous chuckle escapes me, and I wave my hand at him.

"Go ahead."

"Have you had any trouble with Jace since you left?"

I shake my head. "You're the only person I've spoken to from my 'old life,'" I reply using air quotes. "Did you get my letter?"

"I did, and it meant a lot to me. Just so you know." He looks behind him at Jude. "I don't hold anything against you. Even if you would have testified, there was no way I was going to get out of it. The judge had a hard-on for nailing me as soon as the D.A. brought up me being in an MC."

Sounds about right. A small-town judge wanting to throw the book at someone isn't surprising.

There is one question that is still in the back of my mind, though. "This club business, does it have anything to do with me?"

"No." Linc looks at me with confusion. "Why would you think that?" Linc's phone buzzes on the bar before I can answer. He looks down, and I see the name "Ozzy" light up the screen. "Hold on one sec," Linc says as he picks up the phone and walks toward the exit.

"Girl, you two are all kinds of awkward," Lucy says.

My shoulders slump as I look at my best friend. "God, I know. This is so weird. I never expected to run into anyone from my past, especially considering we're in the middle of nowhere, let alone the man who saved me. This is so random." A little too random, if I think about it.

Linc is still on the phone with whoever this Ozzy person is. The patch on his back is tickling a memory somewhere in the back of my mind, but I can't quite grasp it. There's no reason I should know anything about some MC in Massachusetts, but this stubborn feeling won't go away.

He turns to look at me while whoever is on the phone explains something to him. The look isn't what I would call menacing, but it certainly isn't warm, not like the awkward glances we've been giving each other since he walked in. This one is scrutinizing, as though he's trying to work something out in his head.

When Linc ends the call, he looks at the blank screen, then back at me. This time when he approaches, it isn't with the gentle care he was showing in front of Jude. No, this time, there's suspicion in his eyes.

"Are you sure you haven't heard from Jace all this time, Charlie?" he asks, standing in front of me and Lucy with his hands spread on the bar.

"What?" My head rears back at his complete and sudden change in demeanor. "No," I reply, shocked and equally confused.

"What the hell, biker boy?" Lucy asks next to me.

His skeptical gaze swings toward her. "I just got off the phone with my prez. Seems Jace knew about the meeting we had earlier. In fact, he was in town at the same time I was. Told his cousin he was looking for some bitch that fucked him over. Said she stole something that belonged to him."

I can't breathe. Jace knows where I am. Goddammit, I thought I was safe here.

"How do you know that has anything to do with Charlie?" Lucy asks. "That guy sounds like a real piece of shit. Could be a coincidence."

"I don't believe in coincidences, sweetheart." His dark gaze swings to my friend. "That shit can get you killed."

The voice in my head is yelling at me to run. I need to get my shit and get the hell out of town, if not the state entirely. Looking at Lucy, she must see the same look in my eye that she saw all those months ago and nods.

"Alright, boys. It's closing time," she calls.

The two guys playing pool grumble, and Linc's friends look toward the bar.

"What the hell, Lucifer? We just got our beers," Jude calls from the table.

"Fuck that. Charlie, you're going to tell me what the hell's going on," Linc demands.

"If Jace is close, I need to leave," I reply with no room for argument. As Lucy cashes out the other guys, I look Linc square in the eye. "Do you have anything to do with why he's here?"

"Why the hell would I help him find you? Last I knew, he was eating through a straw after I shattered his jaw. What do you have that he wants?"

"What was the MC business you had in Texas?" He needs to answer the damn question. I need to know if this is just some crazy coincidence or if he led him here. "Did it have anything to do with the Irish mob or a man named Cillian?"

"How do you know that name, Charlie?" Linc narrows his eyes. "And what does Jace think you have that he would come find you in Texas?"

"Jace couldn't have found me, Linc." Fear and fire are rolling through me. We need to get everyone out of here, then I'm getting the fuck out, too. "His cousin could, though."

Linc's gaze hardens. "Cillian Doyle is that asshole's cousin?" He leans back from me. "Wow, Charlie. You could have told me that, say, six fucking years ago before I beat the guy up."

"Fucking typical." A disgusted scoff escapes me. "I was the one living in hell, but you wouldn't have done anything had you known Jace was connected, would you? Just like his friends who saw the bruises and did absolutely nothing. They were only concerned with staying on his good side because he has a cousin in the mob."

"Charlie, his cousin, isn't just in the mob. He's the right-hand man of Finnegan Monaghan of the Monaghan family."

Jesus fucking Christ. He has got to be kidding me. Jace never talked much about his cousin, just said they weren't close until about a year before I left. Then he would go on jobs for his cousin but didn't tell me much about what they entailed. I had no idea he was even connected at first until I snuck a peek at the notebook one night when Jace was passed out.

"Fuck," I mutter.

"You can say that again."

When the guys from the pool tables leave the bar, I hear them tell someone walking in that we're closed.

The newcomers don't listen, and three men stand in front of the door.

"Hey, Charlie. Long time no see," Jace sneers.

Double Fuck.

CHAPTER FIVE
LINC

M y head slowly turns toward the voice I was hoping I'd never hear again. I haven't seen this piece of shit since he was sitting in a courtroom six years ago. He looked like hell then and doesn't look much better now.

Jude and the rest of the guys stand from their seats and turn to face Jace and the two goons with him. I don't recognize them from the drop-off, so I assume they weren't part of the Irish crew we met up with earlier. There's no doubt in my mind my prez has no idea Jace is connected to the Irish, so my guess is neither are these guys. Which makes them fair game.

I place myself protectively in front of Charlie. Jace notices, and a wicked smile flits across his face.

"Still the protective asshole from six years ago, I see," Jace starts. "You know, if you think that frigid bitch is gonna give it up to you, you're wasting your time. You could always take it. God knows I had to sometimes." His smile is all teeth when he tries to look around me at the terrified girl I'm attempting to conceal.

The small whimper that escapes Charlie doesn't go unnoticed by me, and the implication of what he just admitted as if it was no big deal fans the flames of angry retribution coursing through me. No woman should ever feel fear like that, especially in my presence.

I see red as I reach under my cut. I've had enough of this disgusting rapist asshole. I should have finished the job years ago. It's time he was put to ground for good.

The movement draws the eyes of the other two assholes with him, and they draw their weapons.

"Get down," I yell to Charlie and Lucy, who are frozen in terror for a brief moment before Jude, Barrett, and Wyatt flip the table onto its side, and the two goons with Jace open fire. I hurl myself over the bar as the bottles behind me explode, raining shards of glass and liquor over the two frightened girls holding tightly to each other. My brothers begin returning fire over the flipped table.

One of Jace's men hollers out in pain and collapses on the floor. These guys are real idiots not having anything they can use for cover before opening fire on a room of bikers. Jace and the other guy go to the injured man on the floor, each grabbing an arm and tumbling outside.

I jump back over the bar and run to the door. Fuck that guy if he thinks he can talk about raping women, then open fire on me and my brothers and get away.

Stepping out into the warm Texas night, I catch the older model sedan peeling out of the gravel parking lot. Raising my gun, I attempt to shoot out the tires or the driver—doesn't matter to me at this point—but the car is swerving so erratically that my bullets miss their target. If I did hit a tire, they're not slowing down to check it out.

When the taillights have disappeared down the dark road, I turn back toward the bar and see my brothers outside with their weapons at their sides.

"They got away," Jude says.

"No shit, Sherlock. Any other studious observations you'd like to share?" Walking back to where my brothers stand, I'm frustrated and angry that, one, I didn't get the license plate, and two, those fuckwads aren't riddled with bullet holes.

"I called Ozzy. He said you had a heads-up that this was a possibility. What other trouble is that girl in there going to bring to our doorstep?" Jude says through a clenched jaw, pointing to the door.

"This is far from her fault, Jude." I say the words, but now I'm not so sure. "And I didn't have time to tell you what Ozzy said before that stupid fuck decided to shoot up the place."

Jude catches the brief flicker of doubt on my face and pounces.

"You don't know that for sure, though, do you? What if he's been holding a grudge all these years and was just waiting to get you away from the rest of the club? Maybe he thinks you knew where Charlie was the entire time, so he's been staking her out, waiting for you to show up and catch you off guard."

My fist tightens around my gun before I put it back in the holster. I might not want to have a deadly weapon in my hand the more shit Jude spouts off about Charlie.

"Or maybe, they've been working together. Maybe he's been here all along, and she called him when you walked into the bar."

"Jude, she was shocked to see him," Barrett interjects. "There's no way you can fake that kind of fear."

When I questioned her about Jace being close, the look on her face hadn't been an act. Nothing Jude says is going to convince me of that, but he does have some valid points. Namely the trouble part. I may not fault her for what happened all those years ago, but I need to know what the hell Jace was talking about. What could be so important that he would track her down to Texas and come in armed and ready to take back whatever she has?

We walk back into the bar and don't see Charlie or Lucy.

"Did they take off?" Wyatt asks behind me. I didn't hear a car or see another set of tail lights, so that's unlikely.

"We're here. Maybe next time you guys walk back into a place after a shootout, you announce yourselves," Lucy says, standing from behind the bar.

Charlie pops up next to Lucy, alcohol and glass shards all over both of them.

While Lucy looks annoyed, she's clearly not as terrified as she was when bullets were flying. Charlie, on the other hand, looks like she's going into shock. Between her pale face, the way she's shaking like a wet kitten, and her gaze darting everywhere and nowhere at once is giving me pause. No, there's no way she could have expected to see him or was working with Jace, as Jude suggested. I doubt he even believed the bullshit he was spewing.

I walk behind the bar and right up to Charlie, placing my palm on her clammy cheek.

"You're okay. He's gone."

She's shaking so hard, her teeth are chattering as she stares at me.

I grab a shot glass and spot a bottle of whisky still intact from the storm of bullets those fuckers rained on us. Grabbing the bottom-shelf whisky and the glass, I pour Charlie a shot. She shakes her head at the offering.

"Trust me, honey, it'll help. You're going into shock."

Lifting her trembling hand to the glass, she grabs it and downs the shot in one go.

Lucy lays her hand on Charlie's back and reaches around with the other, grabbing the bottle from my grasp. She takes a long pull, downing several shots at once. There's no way this girl isn't going to pass the hell out drinking like that.

Jude comes up behind me and grabs the bottle from Lucy's grip.

"That's enough for you, munchkin. I'm not carrying your ass out of here when you pass out."

"Wow. Even after being shot at, you're still a complete dick." Lucy shoots an angry scowl at Jude, who simply shrugs as though he's heard it all before.

"How did he find me?" Charlie asks no one in particular.

"That's what I'd like to know." The suspicion in Jude's voice isn't lost on me.

"We need to get out of here," I tell my brothers. "Who knows if they're coming back for whatever they were looking for in the first place."

Jude looks at Charlie, who's still visibly unsteady.

"What are they after, Charlie?" he asks her.

"I-I don't know," she stammers. Her eyes flicker to Lucy, who's wearing a stone-cold expression, giving nothing away.

"I need to go," Charlie tells Lucy. The two women stare at each other for a few moments, having a silent conversation.

"I agree. You need to come with us," I tell her.

Charlie's eyes dart to me. "I don't want to bring you more trouble."

Jude scoffs, and I shoot him a withering look.

"Listen, we don't know what he's after, and considering who he's connected to, the safest place you can be is with us. Maybe we can convince Cillian to rein in his cousin." And I need to figure out what the hell Charlie has on Jace that almost got us all killed since she doesn't seem inclined to share at the moment. Getting the truth from her is going to take a gentle hand, not angry demands.

Without giving Charlie or Lucy an opportunity to argue, I direct Wyatt to get the van running.

"We'll stop by their place so Charlie can grab her stuff, but we're heading back to Shine tonight."

Lucy steps in front of Charlie. "If you think you're taking her and not me, you're sadly mistaken. Where she goes, I go."

The defiant lift of her chin tells me I don't have a chance in hell of not dragging her along with us. I could probably come up with a plan to make her stay, but I don't have the time, and if it makes Charlie feel safer to have her friend with her, I'm all for it. Maybe if she doesn't feel so scared and defenseless, I can get her to open up to me about what Jace is after and find a way out of this mess.

"Fine," I concede. "But we need to leave now. I'm not waiting around here like a sitting duck."

Charlie's and Lucy's gazes tentatively sweep through the destroyed bar.

"Jimmy is gonna be pissed," Charlie comments as she takes in the broken bottles and bullet holes.

"Not as mad as he'd be if he found two dead bartenders," Wyatt replies with a chuckle.

We all give him a grim look.

"What?" he asks, raising his shoulders as though he doesn't understand how close that was to being a reality.

Shit, if we had gone back to our rooms after eating or decided to stop one town over, this would have ended very differently for Charlie and Lucy.

"Too soon, bro," Barrett tells him, expressing the sentiment we all feel.

"Come on, ladies," I say, not bothering to comment on Wyatt's terrible comedic timing. "Let's get your stuff and get the hell out of here."

Charlie and Lucy grab their shit from behind the bar while my brothers and I head to the door with our guns in hand. Jude opens the door and scans the abandoned street in front of the bar. No one is out at this hour, which tells me no one heard the gunshots inside. I thank our lucky stars there are no red and blue flashing lights waiting for us as Charlie and Lucy emerge from the bar, and we all pile in the van.

"We're going to need new wheels," Barrett says as he starts the engine.

"I'm on it." Jude pulls out his phone to text someone while I pull mine out and call our prez.

"Yeah?" Ozzy answers on the first ring.

"We ran into some trouble. Seems that fucker was closer than we thought."

He lets out a low whistle. "What happened?"

I give him a rundown of the events at the bar.

"What do you need from me?" Ozzy asks.

Jude shows me a text with an address and whispers, "New wheels."

"Nothing at the moment," I reply. "But we're going to have a couple guests for a while."

I don't go into details about why we're bringing the girls back, at least not while they're within hearing distance. Better to explain the situation with all the brothers there at once and get everyone's opinions on how to handle the situation, considering the Irish are likely involved somehow.

"Alright. I'll make sure they have a room, but I want all the details when you get back." With that last order, Ozzy hangs up.

Barrett parks in front of an old bungalow-style house Charlie directs him to.

"We'll only be a second," Charlie tells me before getting out of the van.

My hand gently clasps her arm. "Sweetheart, I'm not letting you go in there until we've checked it out."

Grabbing our weapons, all of us pile out of the van, save for Barrett, who's going to keep it running and keep a lookout while the girls gather their things.

Lucy unlocks the door, allowing Jude and me to enter the house first to have a look around. The last thing we need are unwanted visitors ready and waiting for the girls to come back. As soon as it's clear, we head back to the front door to a waiting Lucy and Charlie.

"All good, but make it quick. We don't know if Jace has your address."

I'm banking on the fact the three assholes who shot up the bar are tending to their friend's gunshot wound, giving us enough time to head out of town without being followed.

"Who did you talk to about getting a new ride?" I ask Jude as the girls go to the back of the house where the bedrooms are.

"My brother."

"Well, shit," I say, raising an eyebrow. "The great Liam Ashcroft really does have contacts all over."

"Yup," Jude huffs.

The Ashcroft brothers aren't particularly close, probably because they're too much alike, both being insufferable pricks on any given day. Liam isn't particularly thrilled with the life Jude leads, and Jude doesn't feel the need to answer to anyone, especially his older brother. Liam certainly comes in handy in a pinch, though. Given his home base is in Philly, I'm surprised his reach stretches to Texas, but I probably shouldn't be. This *is* Liam we're talking about.

"Listen, I know you aren't thrilled with the idea of getting involved with whatever shit Charlie has going on—"

Jude cuts me off with a wave.

"Look, it's not that I think Charlie is the problem. There's no way she was in on this with that fucker, but the way you think you have to be the white knight that comes in to save her is what's concerning. You spent six years in prison, and we were just shot at because of whatever she's hiding. I'm not trying to be a dick here, but I know your mom went through some shit, and you saw a lot of it. I'm just worried you're going to let that cloud your judgment when it comes to her." Jude looks toward the back of the house, where the girls are still gathering their things. "She's hiding something, and I don't want to see it bring down you or the club."

I silently consider his words. There might be some truth to them. Six years ago, it wasn't Jace's face I saw when my fist connected with his face over and over—it was my old man's. Charlie is definitely hiding something—any idiot with half a brain could see that—but whether or not it's going to fuck over me and our club is a risk I have to take.

CHAPTER SIX
CHARLIE

"**Y**ou don't have to go with me," I say for the thousandth time since we've been in my room. I'm throwing as much as I can into two bags while Lucy runs back and forth from her room to mine to make sure I'm okay.

"Uh-uh, sister. I told you family sticks together, so you're stuck with me. Besides, I've never been to Massachusetts." Trying to inject something good in this shit-show that is once again my life, Lucy gives me a wide smile. I return it with a shaky one of my own.

"I still can't believe he found me." A full-body tremor ricochets through me when I think of his smarmy smile and the way he so flippantly brought up our past. "I thought New Orleans would have been far enough away, and when we came to Texas, I never imagined anyone would find me here. We haven't even used our real IDs since coming to town."

Thankfully we had the foresight to spend some decent money on fake IDs when we were in NOLA. Lucy already had one by the time I met her, and fortunately, the guy who made hers was still around. It's amazing what you can find in big cities. Up until then, I'd been lucky enough to find places that let me work under the table, so there was never a paper trail following me.

"Thank God those guys were there. I doubt Billy and his friends would have been able to do much against Jace and his guys."

Lucy makes a good point which reminds me that I still need to call Jimmy and tell him what happened and that Lucy and I are leaving town.

"Yeah, you seemed real grateful for Jude," I tell her with a wry smile.

"That man is an asshole with a capital A. I can't believe he had the audacity to blame you for what happened to Linc."

That's another thing about Lucy—don't ever piss her off. She holds grudges like nobody's business, and once you find yourself on her bad side, good luck.

"He wasn't completely wrong. I did hightail it out of Liberty the second I had the chance and left Linc to deal with the fallout."

"Now listen here, Char." Lucy pins me with a hard look, steely determination brimming in her gaze. "You had no other choice. What would have happened if you had stayed? The second Jace got out of the hospital, he would have found you and probably finished what he was on his way to doing. You'd be dead, Charlie. We both know that. You don't need to explain to anyone your reasons for leaving or take any blame for anything that happened to you. It's horrible that Linc was sentenced at all, considering what Jace was doing to you behind closed doors. But that's the bullshit justice system in a small town for you."

I inhale a deep breath and let it out through my nose, trying to calm myself for the millionth time since seeing Jace's face. This is a similar speech Lucy has given me throughout the few years we've known each other. There's been plenty of nights I regretted not staying and trying to help Linc. Lucy has been there every time to talk me down and try to help me cope with what, for a very long time, I considered some sort of betrayal to Linc.

"Ladies, you about ready?" I hear an accented voice call from the living room.

Lucy rolls her eyes at the interruption while I zip up my bag, then we head to the other bedroom to grab the rest of her things.

When I grab the notebook, I'm reminded of the weird almost-memory I had in the bar before Jace showed up. There was something pulling at me when I saw the patch on Linc's cut. I open the notebook and scan its contents. There are notes with dates, times, and addresses. Some of it Jace wrote using only initials. One that stands out is BR and the initial O and T.

Knowing what I do about motorcycle clubs, I wonder if that stands for Black Roses, especially considering Linc seems to know who Jace's cousin is. This is info Jace collected while doing odd jobs for his cousin I hardly knew anything about. The only thing he told me about his cousin was that he's connected. Jace liked to brag about it. He enjoyed telling me I could disappear from the face of the Earth, and no one would find me because of who his cousin was. I only met the man once, and he didn't exactly strike me as the friendly type, so I had no reason to doubt Jace. Then when I saw him in New Orleans, I could only assume Jace was going to make good on his threat.

Now looking over the initials, I can't help but question if I'm walking into the lion's den by going with Linc. Though he's never been anything but protective toward me, there's no telling what his club would do if they knew I had information about their deals with the Irish.

"You ready, sweetie?" Lucy asks from my doorway.

I slam the book shut and shove it to the bottom of my bag. I'm probably overthinking this. The initials could be anything. Who's to say Jace's cousin even knows about this notebook? My guess is it would get Jace in a lot more trouble with the wrong people if he ever found out.

"Yup, let's go," I call back, grabbing my bag and slinging it over my shoulder. Right now, my priority is getting the hell out of town.

Our next stop is the hotel where the guys had planned on staying the night. It takes them about two minutes before they're on their bikes and we're heading north.

Watching Linc on his motorcycle as we speed down the highway is truly a sight. He looks one with the machine between his thighs as the engine growls and rumbles. I've never even ridden with someone on a bike. The effortless ease of the way he handles the machine is hypnotizing. He and his brothers maintain a triangle in front of the van Lucy and I are riding in, as if they've been doing it their entire lives. Every turn we make reminds me of a flock of birds in the sky, never breaking formation.

After about two hours and crossing into Arkansas, the guys exit the highway and drive through another sleepy little town similar to the one we just left. It takes thirty minutes on a dirt road before we come to a stop. The headlights shine on a man standing in front of a barn, waving to us. Jude is the first off his bike and walks up to him, shaking his hand, then motioning for us to get out of the van. The older man, who I would guess would rather be sleeping at this hour than dealing with us, opens the large door.

Linc walks to Lucy and me as we take a minute to stretch after being in the van for the last few hours.

"We're switching out vehicles," he tells me. "How are you feeling?"

That's a loaded question I have a million different answers for.

"Tired, but good," I reply, offering a small smile. Best to keep my answer as benign as possible for the time being.

Linc takes a minute to look me over as though he's making sure for himself. Once he seems satisfied I'm not going to drop from shock like earlier, he reaches into the van and pulls the few bags Lucy and I brought with us.

"Come on, I'll put these in the new ride, then we'll be on our way."

"You must have some pretty good friends if they don't mind being woken up at this unholy hour to help you guys out," Lucy quips as we make our way to the barn.

"Friend of Jude's brother. The MC has a pretty long reach, but not as long as Liam's."

"Is Jude's brother in the MC, too?" I ask.

"No," Linc laughs and shakes his head. "He runs a security firm in Philly."

"Is he the nice one?" Lucy asks as Jude makes his way to us.

"Aw, Lucifer, are you saying I'm not nice?" Jude rests his hand over his heart. "I'm devastated."

Lucy rolls her eyes before opening the car door and slamming it shut. Jude lets out a boisterous laugh while Barrett and I make ourselves comfortable in the front seat.

"Come on, let's get out of here so Jasper can get some sleep before morning chores," Jude tells the group.

The smaller sedan is less roomy than the giant van but probably less conspicuous. We get back to the highway and once again, follow the formation of motorcycles leading us east. The steady roar of the bikes and the gentle rocking of the car as we head down the highway is enough to make my eyelids droop. Even though I have a million questions about what I'm about to walk into once we get to Massachusetts, I can't fight the exhaustion from overtaking me. I fall into an uneasy sleep, my dreams plaguing me with images of blood and glass reigning down on me while Jace stalks toward me, that evil smirk I saw so many times on his face, telling me I'll never be free.

After what seems like a hundred hours on the road but, in reality, was about twelve, we pull off the highway and find a little motel. So far, we've only stopped for gas and to grab snacks so we could all stretch our legs. Lucy and I have been sleeping on and off, but both of us are exhausted and stiff as hell. It doesn't take much to imagine how Linc and the rest of the guys riding must feel right about now.

Barrett goes to the office and comes back with three room keys.

"You two are sharing a room. We'll stop here for the night. Let's get settled, then grab some grub."

The three rooms are lined up next to each other around the back of the motel in front of the kidney-shaped pool that's seen better days.

"Girl, I am in desperate need of a hot shower and to brush my dang teeth. I'm pretty sure they're wearing sweaters at this point," Lucy says, opening the door to our room.

I laugh as she throws her stuff on the bed.

"I'll let you go first."

When I turn around, I see Linc head into the room next to ours. When his tired gaze lands on mine, I give him a small smile.

"We'll rest, then get something from the diner across the street, yeah?" he asks, opening his door.

"Sounds good."

Closing the door to our room, I lean against it while Lucy pulls her things from her bag and heads to the bathroom. The image of Linc's soft hazel eyes imprints on the back of my lids, and his soft voice from that night in the truck comes back to me.

I don't regret a thing.

I can't help wondering if he'll still feel that way when he realizes what I stole from Jace that night almost got us all killed. Or if he'll decide my baggage is too much and wash his hands of me when we get to his clubhouse.

Lucy comes out of the bathroom while I'm still leaning against the door.

"Damn girl, are you so tired that you fell asleep standing up?" she jokes, running a brush through her long black hair.

"No, just lost in thought."

"Those thoughts have anything to do with a certain biker you've barely been able to keep your eyes off for the last twelve hours we were in the car?"

Lucy sees too damn much. Instead of answering her, I heave off the door and grab a change of clothes, heading to the bathroom. The door shuts on Lucy's laugh.

"Busted," she sing-songs through the thin wood.

I've just finished braiding my wet hair after my shower and thinking it's about time to grab a bottle of dye to darken my roots again when there's a knock on the door. Lucy opens it after checking the peephole, and I hear Linc's rough voice.

"We're headed out to get some food. You ladies still up for joining us?"

I must be high from sleep deprivation or something because when he speaks, I can almost feel the rumble of his voice roll through me. Lucy turns to me while I'm still lost in my reaction to the sound of Linc's deep timbre. I shake out of my stupor and nod.

"Yeah," I croak out. "Sounds good."

"Be out in a minute," she tells him, then looks back at me. "You okay?"

"Yup, just tired."

The look Lucy sends me says she doesn't buy it but thankfully, stays silent.

When we walk out, the sun is still high in the sky, and the four bikers are there, freshly showered and waiting for us. They're all wearing their cuts, and I watch as a car full of women probably my age passes the parking lot in front of the motel. The way all of them, including the driver, stare at these guys has my hackles rising. Jesus, I'm surprised they didn't run into the little old lady walking her dog down the sidewalk. The guys, of course, don't notice.

"Good God, please smack me if I'm ever that obvious checking out a man," Lucy comments with an eye roll.

We laugh as we walk arm in arm to where the guys are standing.

"What's so funny over there?" Wyatt asks.

"Wouldn't you like to know," Lucy sasses. The last thing any of these guys probably need is an ego boost.

Linc comes to my other side as the three other bikers walk in front of us to cross the street to the little diner that reminds me so much of where I first met Linc.

"She's gonna be a problem, isn't she?" he asks, nodding to Lucy.

Chuckling, I say, "You have no idea." My best friend is a force to be reckoned with.

"You scared of little ol' me, biker boy?" Lucy drawls, batting her eyelashes at Linc.

Jude holds the door for the three of us to walk through, chuckling under his breath. "I have a feeling you're all bark and no bite, Lucifer."

"We'll see about that." Lucy smiles sweetly before snapping her jaws at him.

Lucy saunters to a table, putting a little extra sway in her hips. She may be short, but her curves had the men in NOLA and Texas panting after her like thirsty dogs.

"I wouldn't be too sure about the no-bite thing, Jude. I've seen her make grown men cry with one well-placed knee shot to their dicks," I warn.

Jude looks from me to Lucy, then back to me with an expression that's difficult to decipher. Maybe cautious curiosity?

"Noted."

The six of us sit in a large circular booth in the back of the restaurant. I'm wedged between Lucy and Linc, who is sitting on the edge of the booth with his long legs eating up the tight space under the table. It's not like he can help his thigh pressing into mine, but that doesn't stop my heart from trying to beat out of my chest at the contact. I'm attempting to read the menu to decide what I want for dinner, but my mind keeps wandering to the heat radiating from his thigh to mine.

"What looks good to you?" Linc asks, way too close to me for me to be able to concentrate on anything other than the way his warm, minty breath fans against my face.

"Burger," I blurt. "With bacon."

A wide smile lights Linc's face. "I like a girl who appreciates meat."

"Oh, yeah, I'm all about the meat." What am I even saying?

After the waitress comes to take our order, the conversation resumes around the table, thankfully distracting me from the feel of Linc's body brushing against mine.

Well, almost.

Lucy is talking up a storm, telling the guys funny stories from all the different places she's worked across the country. She comes from a little town in Nevada she swears no one has ever heard of, so she never tells anyone where it is. At least, that's what she says. I think her being tight-lipped about where she's from is a little more involved.

When we get our food, my eyes bulge out of my head, seeing the size of my burger.

"Dang girl, you're going to have to unhinge your jaw to fit that beast," Lucy says.

Linc chokes on his drink next to me, and Barrett and Wyatt laugh so loud, a couple of the other patrons jump at the booming noise.

I shoot Lucy a shut-the-hell-up stare, and she shrugs.

Do all bikers have a sixteen-year-old boy's sense of humor?

After stuffing our faces without anyone having to unhinge anything, thank you very much, we make our way back to the motel. Though it's only about six in the evening, we're all exhausted.

The second my head hits the pillow, I fall into a blissfully dreamless sleep.

CHAPTER SEVEN
UNC

My brothers and I haven't slept for over twenty-four hours. When we return to the motel, Jude flops face first onto his bed and soon, there's loud snoring coming from his side of the room. It takes me a little longer than thirty seconds to fall asleep. My mind is still racing with the events of the day.

Charlie is hiding something, there's no doubt in my mind. Whether it has to do with the club or only with Jace is yet to be determined. Considering how Jace is intertwined with the club because of his cousin, it means anything having to do with him will undoubtedly affect the club somehow. Fuck, this is not a complication I want to deal with.

The idea of Charlie not feeling as though she can confide in me and trust me to protect her doesn't sit right. Neither do the feelings I was having at dinner. I shouldn't be thinking about what her mouth looked like while chewing her food or the little moans she let out when she took that first bite of her burger, as if she had never tasted something so delicious. And I definitely shouldn't be imagining other things that she could put in her mouth that would make her moan like that. The way the heat from her thigh spread into mine while we were sitting next to each other in the booth also shouldn't be playing on repeat through my tired brain.

When the gray matter between my ears finally slows down enough for the exhaustion to take over my body, blue eyes and dark hair haunt my dreams. They aren't the same sad eyes I dreamt about in prison. These ones are rimmed in smokey black liner and looking at me with heated desire.

Waking with a start, I jolt up in bed, disoriented and breathing fast. Sometimes, I have the sinking feeling I'm still locked in prison with my cellmate snoring above me. It takes me the span of a breath to remember I'm in a motel in some little no-name town, and the snoring I hear is Jude, still asleep in the bed next to mine.

The shot of adrenaline coursing through me means I won't be getting any more shut-eye anytime soon. Instead of tossing and turning like I usually do, I decide to get some fresh air. On nights like this, walking outside and seeing the starry sky helps ground me, reminding me I'm not still in a six-by-eight cell.

After throwing on a pair of jeans and grabbing the pack of smokes I keep on hand out of habit more than anything, I make my way to the pool area of the rundown motel. It's after the posted open hours but the lock on the flimsy gate is broken. There're a few loungers set up and a couple tables surrounding the small, kidney-shaped pool that's probably seen better days.

Lighting my first cigarette of the day, my sore ass plops down on one of the old plastic chairs. I inhale the smoke into my lungs and let out a long breath as the nicotine rushes through my bloodstream.

God, this is all such a cluster fuck. We have about twelve more hours of driving before we're back in Shine. That's twelve more hours on my bike with nothing to keep me company other than the thoughts racing through my mind. I have no idea what Ozzy and the rest of the brothers are going to say about the shitstorm we've found ourselves in or rather the one I've put us in with, once again, taking on Charlie's problems. There was no way I could have walked away last night, knowing her ex was after her. I couldn't do it six years ago, and it cost me my freedom.

Makes me wonder what it's going to cost me this time.

"I didn't know you smoked."

The soft voice startles me from my thoughts. I turn to see the dark-haired beauty that starred in my dreams just minutes ago at the gate.

"I don't."

Charlie lets out a breathy laugh that hits me in my chest.

"The lit cigarette in your hand says otherwise."

I look at the cigarette smoke curling through the air. "Huh. How did that get there?"

Charlie shakes her head, and a small smile tips up the corner of her mouth.

"Come have a seat with me," I tell her, patting the lounger next to me.

She opens the broken gate and lies down next to me, looking up at the stars.

"Why are you awake?" she asks turning her gaze to me. "I thought for sure you would be passed out cold like everyone else."

I shrug a shoulder, taking one last hit from my cigarette before stubbing it out.

"Sleeping isn't always easy to come by these days."

Charlie's gaze softens in understanding. I'm sure she's had plenty of those nights herself.

"What about you?"

"Would you believe Lucy snores like a truck driver after thirty-six hours on the road?"

I think about it for a moment and shake my head. "No. Try again."

Charlie lets out a deep sigh and tilts her head back to the stars.

"Guilt, fear, the never-ending pit of doom I feel in my gut." She waves a hand toward the sky. "Take your pick."

A puff of air leaves my lips. "That's a lot to unpack there, Charlie girl."

She startles at my nickname. "Nope," she says, holding up her index finger. "That sounds like you're calling a dog."

A laugh tumbles from my lips. "Noted. I'll work on it."

Charlie nods and responds in a prim voice. "Thank you."

A couple beats of silence pass before I speak again. "Why the guilt?"

"What's not to feel guilty about?" She lets out a humorless laugh. "I've dragged my best friend across the country with me out of some sense of loyalty on her part, putting her life in danger. I've dragged you and your club into another mess with Jace and come to find out, the Irish mob as well. And once again, you're taking the role of protector for someone you barely know. Last time you did that, you went to prison." Charlie lets out another sigh. "So, yeah, I feel guilty."

I consider all of her points before I hold up a finger of my own.

"First, Lucy is here because she's fierce and loyal to you. That's the kind of shit I've only seen with my brothers." I hold up another finger. "Second, my club is involved with a lot of shit, but I'll tell you right now, there isn't a single one of us who would stand by and let a piece of shit like your ex attack you and threaten your life while we sat back and watched just because the Irish are involved. It isn't in our DNA, sweetheart." I hold up a third finger. "And third, when you live the kind of life I do, prison is always a possibility." Charlie opens her mouth to argue. "No, Charlie. There was always a chance I would go to prison for something club related. It's a chance we all take, and we're all prepared for it. I did what I did that night for more reasons than what he did to you."

She gives me a small nod in understanding while she absorbs everything I just told her.

"I hope one of these days you'll tell me," she says softly, looking back at the stars.

"One of these days, I will."

Charlie bites her lip, and it takes everything in me not to reach over and pull it from her teeth.

"I also wanted to apologize for what I said at the bar."

My brows draw down with confusion at her statement.

She turns her head and locks her gaze with mine. "When I said you wouldn't have helped me if you would have known who Jace's cousin was. I know that's not true."

I'd forgotten about that little dig, but the reminder brings back the sting I felt. It's true what I said to her. No one in my club would sit back and let a man beat on a woman just because of business ties. It's sad to think that's all she had known when she was with Jace.

"Don't sweat it, angel."

Charlie sends me a questioning look.

"Like Charlie's Angels, because, you know." I wave my hand in her direction.

"That's even worse than the first," she replies, rolling her eyes again.

"I'll work on it some more."

"Or, and this is just a thought, you just call me Charlie."

"Nah, this is more fun."

"Lord, help me." She laughs, looking toward the dark sky as she rises from the lounger. "I'm going to go back to my room and try to get a little more sleep before we leave."

I smile at her as she stretches her arms over her head, the thin tank she's wearing riding above her sleep shorts, showing a small sliver of soft skin. A sudden and almost feral urge to trace my lips against her smooth flesh takes me by surprise before I tamp it down. The last thing this girl needs is an ex-con biker pawing at her.

"We'll be leaving in a few hours. I think all of us will feel better once we're back at the clubhouse." Clearing my throat, I attempt to clear my mind at the same time.

Charlie nods and heads back to the pool gate. "See you in the morning," she calls, holding up her hand and waving before disappearing around the corner.

The ride back to Shine was grueling. Instead of taking the back roads as we did on the way to Texas, it was decided we would take the most direct route, which meant a lot of time on crowded highways, breathing in exhaust fumes and dodging minivans.

None of us were sure how Jace found us in Texas or if he was after us at all. It could have been his cousin, or he could have been looking for Charlie and assumed we would lead him to her. I don't know if or how long he's been following the club, but the sooner we're back in Shine, the better.

Pulling into the club's compound after twelve hours of riding has me breathing a sigh of relief. Being in the open like we had been had us all on edge, but now that we're in the safety of these gates, we can finally figure out what our next move is.

"You made good time," I hear Ozzy call as I'm moving my stiff legs off my bike.

He crosses the gravel lot and reaches out to clasp my hand.

"We weren't stopping for shit," I reply, releasing his grip and stretching my arms over my head.

Ozzy lets out a chuckle at my obvious discomfort. "You'll be paying for that decision for the next couple days."

"Worth it to see your pretty mug."

Ozzy's laugh is deep and loud.

"I doubt it's my face you want to see."

He's probably talking about one of the club bunnies, but the only face I see in my mind is Charlie's. Though we traveled from Texas together, she wasn't on my bike. Lucy and Charlie opted to ride in the car with Barrett, which was fine by me. I don't want her on the back of my bike while she's scared that her deranged ex could show up any minute. No, the first time she's on my bike, I want her to love it as much as I do. Not that I thought about her being glued to my back instead of in the car for most of the ride.

Nope, not at all.

When Ozzy walks over to the rest of the guys to check in, I head to the car and open the door for Charlie. She greets me with a tired smile as she takes my offered hand and slowly gets out.

"Such a gentleman."

"I don't know if that's a word I would use to describe myself."

The truth is I couldn't go another second without putting eyes on her. I needed to see for myself that she felt safe and wasn't regretting her decision to come back to Shine.

"This must be Charlie," Ozzy says from behind me.

Charlie looks at the giant of a man and clasps my hand a little tighter. The urge to pull her behind me and protect her from feeling any sort of anxiety when she meets Ozzy catches me off guard. There's nothing for her to fear from my president, but anyone making Charlie feel uncomfortable doesn't sit right with me.

Fuck, I need to get my shit together. Exhaustion from our trip and everything that went down is fucking with my head.

Ozzy holds out a hand and offers it to Charlie. She shakes it without letting go of mine. That little tidbit doesn't escape Ozzy's scrutinizing gaze.

"Thank you for letting me and Lucy come stay with you guys."

Just then, Lucy gets out of the car, and a loud groan escapes her as she stretches her arms high above her head.

"Thank God. I thought I was going to become one with the seat if I was in that car another second." Lucy bends over to stretch her back, and every guy behind her is staring at her ass while she's completely unaware of the show she's giving my brothers. Naturally, Jude takes the opportunity to call out a lewd comment.

"Fuck you, asshole," she calls back to him.

"Anytime, darling. I'd love to see what other positions you can twist yourself into." He shoots her a lecherous smile.

She holds up her middle finger toward him.

Ozzy watches the exchange with curiosity. "I see Jude is making friends wherever he goes."

"He does have a way with the ladies," I reply as Lucy makes her way over to us.

"Is that what you call it?" she asks. Lucy reaches her hand to Ozzy. "Hi, I'm Lucy." Ozzy shakes it. "Your brother is a pig."

Ozzy laughs and nods his head. "Tell me something I don't know, sweetheart." He releases her grasp and turns toward the clubhouse. "Come on in. Let's get you girls settled."

Charlie is quiet as she walks to the clubhouse, taking in the building and the few brothers mingling around.

"You okay, Charlie bug?"

She and Lucy give me a surprised and slightly disgusted look.

"That one might be worse than the last two you tried," Charlie says.

"Did you just call her a bug?" Lucy asks.

"I've been trying out nicknames," I say with a smile.

"And failing miserably," Charlie adds when we walk through the door.

As soon as I enter, Stacia runs up to me and throws her arms around my neck.

"I'm so glad you're back. I've missed you, baby," she croons.

Charlie rips her hand from my grasp, and Stacia catches the movement.

"I heard you were bringing a couple stragglers back," Stacia says as she looks Charlie over in a not-so-friendly manner.

"I'm Stacia. Linc's... friend." The way she says 'friend' with her hand sliding over my stomach leaves no room for misinterpretation. Unfortunately for Stacia, she seems to be the one who's misinterpreted what she is to me.

Charlie plasters a fake smile on her face. "I'm Charlie, and this is Lucy," she says, waving in her friend's direction.

Stacia ignores the introduction and rises on her tiptoes to kiss my cheek. "I'm so glad you're finally back. It's been so boring here without you."

I grasp Stacia's biceps and firmly pull her arms from around me, causing her to take a step back.

"Stacia, why don't you show Charlie and Lucy to a room? Then grab a couple of the other girls and see about scrounging up some dinner. We're all starved." I look at Charlie, who's wearing a blank expression. "I need to talk to Ozzy and the other brothers, but I'll come find you when we're done."

The tight smile I get in return tells me all I need to know about her reaction to Stacia's wandering hands.

"Come on, Carly and Lisa." Stacia turns on her too-high heels with a huff. "I'm sure we can find you somewhere to get cleaned up," she says, looking at the girls with her nose scrunched as though she smells something foul.

"It's Charlie and Lucy," Charlie grits out, staring daggers at an obviously jealous woman.

"Oops. My mistake," Stacia replies with a snotty tone.

Fuck me, this is going to be another problem we don't need right now.

After the girls follow Stacia, I go in search of Ozzy. He's back in his office going over some paperwork when I knock on the doorframe.

"Girls find a room?"

"Yup, I have Stacia showing them one now."

"Great. Church starts in five. You can grab a beer and meet us in there. I wanna know everything that went down."

Going back to the main room, I belly up to the bar. The prospect manning it slides me a bottle, and I nod in thanks. Goddamn, I'm tired as hell and want nothing more than my bed and a full eight hours of sleep, but the club needs to know what's going on, and I'd rather only tell the story once.

Inhaling a deep breath, I head toward the back of the building where we hold church. My brothers are already seated at the large wooden table with the Black Roses insignia carved in the center. I take my chair next to Jude, and Ozzy bangs the gavel on the wood signaling for us all to shut up.

"Alright, boys. Seems some shit went down in Texas." He tilts his head in my direction, and I take over.

I tell them about seeing Charlie again and Jace coming into the bar while we were there.

"Seems he thinks she has something of his, and he wants it back," I explain.

"What is it?" Knox, our VP and my actual blood brother, asks from his seat next to Ozzy.

"Not sure. She seemed confused about what he was talking about. The guy has obviously been using. He looked worse than when I had my run-in with him six years ago."

"Yeah, and look where that got you," Braxton, our Sergeant-At-Arms, supplies helpfully.

"Look I'm not saying I didn't bring a whole bag of trouble back with me, but what the hell was I supposed to do? The guy came in, guns blazing. I wasn't about to leave Charlie and Lucy because shit went sideways six years ago. There was no way, brother." I couldn't leave her the first time, and I sure as shit wasn't about to leave her now.

"There's one more thing." Here comes the part that's really going to ruffle some feathers. "Cillian Doyle is Jace's cousin."

Cash, our club's treasurer, lets out a long whistle through his teeth. "Fuck." He's probably thinking about all the ways this could screw with our income.

A few of the brothers nod in understanding and a few more swipe their palms over their faces, their thoughts most likely headed in the same direction as Cash's. The deal with the Irish has proven to be extremely beneficial for all of our bank accounts.

Ozzy leans back after I finish explaining the events of that night and contemplates the predicament we may have just found ourselves in.

"Alright. Obviously, this fuckwit being tied with the Irish complicates a few things. We need to know what he was after. Was it just a case of wounded pride, or does she have something that could take him or his cousin down? Linc," he says, turning to me. "Are you willing to take responsibility for the girl and her friend 'til we get this straightened out?"

Jude scoffs next to me at the mention of Charlie's friend.

"I've got it covered, Oz," I reply.

"Great. You and Jude are on Charlie and Lucy duty until we figure a way to sift through this shitstorm."

Jude's head swings toward Ozzy. "Why me?" he groans.

"One, because Linc is your brother, and he needs the help." Ozzy's lips tip up in a devious smirk. "And two, I just like torturing you."

Laughter roars from the brothers as Linc lets out a suffering sigh.

Ozzy slams the gavel on the wooden table once again, dismissing us from church. We all file out and head to the bar.

"Shot?" I ask Jude as he plops himself on the stool next to me.

"Yeah." he nods. "Better make it a bottle," my overly dramatic best friend says, grabbing the whiskey from the prospect's hand.

This is going to be an interesting couple of weeks.

CHAPTER EIGHT
CHARLIE

"This is the only room we have available right now. Hope it's up to your standards," Stacia sneers in my direction.

The room is perfectly fine. A little dated, sure, with two twin beds and an old nightstand separating them, but it has a TV and a private bathroom, so I'm certainly not going to complain.

"It's perfect. I probably won't be spending much time in here, anyway," I say back to her with a shit-eating grin on my face. I have no intention of staying anywhere else, but I'm exhausted on every level and sick of her attitude.

"Yeah, thanks, Stacy, you've just been so welcoming," Lucy says in a dry-as-hell voice.

"It's Stacia."

"Sure it is, sweetie," my friend replies.

Lucy snickers next to me when Stacia turns on her heel, flips her bottle-blonde extensions over her shoulders, and walks out of the room without sparing either of us another glance.

As soon as the door closes, Lucy and I collapse onto one of the beds and start giggling like schoolgirls. It feels good to laugh through this clusterfuck of a situation.

"Damn, friend, what got into you? That bitch practically peed on him in front of us, and you were having none of it." She continues laughing as I let out a groan.

"I feel kind of bad. What if that's his girlfriend?"

"I believe bikers call them old ladies," Lucy replies, scrunching up her nose. "But I don't think she's either, if his reaction is anything to go by. He couldn't get her hands off him fast enough."

"It doesn't matter." I shake my head. "I'm literally the last person he should even consider having any type of relationship with."

"Woah, girl. What the fuck? Who was talking about a relationship?" Lucy squints her eyes and cocks her head to the side. "What was all that about a nickname earlier?" she asks, suspicion lacing her tone.

"Nothing." I wave my hand at her, rolling my eyes. "It was something he did last night."

"When last night?"

"Jesus, what's with the third degree?" I laugh to try to cover my frayed nerves, but it's no use. Lucy has known me long enough and well enough to see through my bullshit.

Lucy stays silent, staring at me as though she has the power to read my mind or get me to spill the beans with that look alone.

Oh, who am I kidding? She totally does.

"I couldn't sleep last night, so I was going to sit by the pool for a bit to clear my head. Linc was out there, and we talked for a while."

"And by talked, you mean..."

"Talked. Then he decided to try out a couple nicknames that were absolutely terrible." I smile, remembering his failed attempts.

"Okay, what's that look?" Lucy asks, pointing at my face.

"What look? There's no look."

"Oh no, you don't. You had one of those dreamy looks in your eyes. Are you catching feelings for the biker?"

Squeezing my eyes shut, I decide to be as honest as possible.

"Maybe. No. Ugh, I don't know." I look at Lucy, who has an 'I told you so' smile on her face.

"It's a little more complicated than a simple crush on a guy I met in a bar, don't you think?"

Lucy tilts her head back and forth before blowing out a breath.

"Yes, but all of this will be over soon. Then you two can see where anything between you can go. I mean, it's not like any guy in the five years I've known you has caught your eye. And I've definitely never seen you this flustered over any man."

"Assuming we make it out of this without him hating me. You heard him at the bar. One of the top guys in the Irish mob is Jace's cousin, and I happen to have information on said cousin, who also has dealings with Linc's MC. Information I'm sure I shouldn't know and could probably get me killed. And once again, I'm putting Linc, and now his entire club, in the middle of my mess." I scrub my hands over my face and peer at Lucy through my fingers.

"What part of that screams, now's a good time to explore feelings with someone who spent time in prison for beating the hell out of the ex who used to beat the hell out of me?"

"Well, when you put it like that." Lucy laughs as I smack her on the side of the head with the thin-as-hell pillow Stacia laid on the bed for us.

"Regardless of whether or not you have any intention of pursuing anything with the hot biker next door, I loved seeing you put that bitch in her place," Lucy says, referring to the blonde harpy.

"There was just something about the way she pawed at him, then looked at me like I was the dirt on the bottom of her stripper heels that didn't sit well."

"There was nothing about that girl that sat right with me," Lucy replies with an exaggerated full-body shiver.

"It doesn't matter. Linc isn't mine and never will be. As soon as they figure out the shit I've been keeping from them, the entire club will want us gone... including Linc."

"Why do you think that?"

"When I saw their cuts, it snagged a memory from something in the notebook. There were a couple entries with coordinates and the initials BR and O and T. I'm not sure if it means Black Roses or what O and T stand for. O could be Ozzy, I guess, but I don't know about T."

Lucy hums while mulling over the information I just shared with her. "Honestly, Char, that could mean anything. You may be making connections that aren't there."

"True," I concede. "But considering Linc knows Jace's cousin, it's not a stretch to think the club has had dealings with him. Not like these guys are squeaky clean."

I realize it's possible I'm making a mountain out of a molehill, but I haven't survived this long by not considering all possibilities, whether they seem based in fact to other people. I'll never again allow myself to be in the same situation I ran from the night Linc was arrested.

"Why did you agree to come here if you were scared the club is somehow involved with the stuff in that notebook?"

That's a great question, and the answer makes me sound like a starry-eyed girl lusting over the one man in her life who ever gave a shit about what was happening to her. But it's the truth.

"There's something about Linc that makes me want to trust him. It's completely and totally at odds with who I know him to be. He's a biker who deals with the mob. He had no problem with almost killing a man all those years ago." I think back to that night and the moment I put my hand on his shoulder when he had Jace broken and bloody on the floor. "Honestly, Lucy, if I didn't stop him, there's no doubt in my mind he would have killed Jace."

"It's not like the world *wouldn't* have been better off without that scumbag breathing."

I nod in agreement. She's not wrong.

"When the cops showed up and he knew he was going to jail, I thought about the way his hand felt against my cheek when he told me he didn't regret it. It's the first time in so long I was touched with any sort of gentleness. It's like my brain short-circuited, and he became this unobtainable savior."

"Babe, you were starved for affection. It's no wonder you felt that way."

"Exactly. Which is why I don't trust these feelings that keep popping up when it comes to him. The last six years, I've held him on a pedestal instead of looking at the reality of the situation. I can't let myself do that. He's just a man and a seemingly dangerous one at that." I don't know who I'm trying to convince here, me or Lucy.

"Anyway, that's why I agreed to come back with him. That, and I doubt Jace is stupid enough to storm a compound full of bikers. We just need to lie low for a minute and figure out where we can go. Now that Jace attacked members of the club, he's in their crosshairs. I think the best thing to do is wait for the dust to settle, then take off. They can deal with Jace, and we can start over."

Lucy looks at me for a few beats before speaking.

"That sounds good in theory, but are you sure you can start over without looking back and questioning whether Linc could have been more than just someone you put on a pedestal?"

"Woah there, sister. Now who's talking about relationships? I have no intention of sticking around, and I doubt anyone here wants me to." Just remembering the way Jude looked at me at the bar sends shivers down my spine. If I thought the greeting from Stacia was cold, the icy glare in Jude's eyes made me want to run right out of that bar.

"Ozzy seemed nice enough," Lucy says.

"He's one guy."

"Are you talking about that smashole Jude?"

A sudden laugh escapes me. "Smashole?"

"Yeah, as in he's an asshole, but I'd totally smash that. Even I can't deny he's sexy as hell with that accent and all."

"Oh my God, Lucy, I can't believe you just said that."

She looks at me like I've lost my mind. "Really?"

I think about it for a moment. "Wait. Yeah, I totally can."

We're laughing when a knock sounds from the other side of the door. Linc pops his head in and smiles at the two of us lying on the tiny twin bed.

"Man, if Jude could see you now," he says.

Footsteps pound down the hallway, and I hear Jude call, "See what? What's going on in there?" The door swings all the way open as the British biker surveys the room. "Oh, bollocks. There's nothing exciting here. They both have their clothes on, for chrissake."

"Get out of here, you fucking perv," Lucy yells, throwing a pillow at him.

"You sure, love?" Jude asks, crossing his arms and leaning against the doorframe while shooting her a wicked grin. "We could remedy the lack of nudity in no time if I stay."

Lucy pops up into a sitting position and points at him. "Out. Now."

Linc puts a hand on Jude's chest and pushes him out the door.

"I just wanted to let you know the food will be ready soon. We're having a bit of a celebration since we just got back from a run, so it might get a little rowdy," Linc warns.

"Sweetheart, me and this girl have been working in bars for the last five years. Trust me, we can handle rowdy," Lucy replies.

"What else do you think you can handle?" Jude asks, looking Lucy over.

"Wouldn't you like to know," she tells him, batting her eyelashes dramatically. "Now, get the hell out of our room."

Linc shakes his head at the ridiculous ribbing between his best friend and mine before focusing his gaze on me.

"If you want to eat in your room, I'd completely understand."

"I'm good. We'll meet you out there in a few." I offer him a small smile before he closes the door behind him.

"See," Lucy starts. "Smashole."

Dinner is a casual affair. Apparently, none of these guys cook for themselves, so what I've come to know as club bunnies make their meals for them. If Stacia has anything to do with it, I can only pray she hasn't poisoned my food.

We get a few curious stares from the bikers. Nothing that makes me feel uncomfortable, but I can tell they're wondering how we're going to react to being in a clubhouse full of bikers. Especially if things get wild, as Linc warned. The bunnies, on the other hand, are a different story. There's downright hostility in their eyes when any of them look at me or Lucy. I guess Stacia didn't have the nicest things to say about us to her friends. Shocker.

After dinner, Lucy and I go back to our room to lie down. The last two days have taken it out of me, to say the least. Linc looked a little too relieved when I told him Lucy and I were going to bow out of tonight's festivities. I'm glad he's home with his brothers, but I'd be lying to myself if I didn't admit it cut a little when I saw that look on his face.

Lying in bed, I'm enjoying one of the books I grabbed from our house before coming to Shine. I need to get out of my head and into a fictional world right now.

"Do you want to go out there and see what all the fuss is about?" Lucy asks from her bed.

"What fuss?" I ask, looking away from my book. Generally, the answer to that question is no, especially considering I just got to the part in my book when they first kiss. I'm a sucker for those, considering I haven't had a first kiss in what feels like forever.

"A biker party," she responds.

"I doubt we're missing much, but if you want to go, I'll come with you."

I don't know much about parties in a biker compound, but I know they can get out of control, at least if the television shows I've watched are true.

The drinking began before dinner. At this point, everyone except us are at least two sheets to the wind if not the full three.

I've never stepped foot inside a biker compound, but have plenty of experience working in bars, watching all the drunks make fools of themselves and do things that had they been sober would have never crossed their minds. This is similar but turned up about seventeen notches. And I doubt any of these guys would have a problem doing half this shit sober.

The women here are wearing fewer clothes than any of the people who came into the bar where we used to work, like a lot less. I didn't realize there was a way to make jean shorts look like underwear, and Victoria has no secrets in this place. Apparently, they even have girls here from the strip club the MC owns for entertainment, according to the conversation I heard walking to the bar. I'll say one thing, the rules that I've heard are enforced in a strip club don't apply here.

We try not to look like a deer in headlights, but it's not easy, considering I've never been to a strip club, and this looks like one on steroids. I'm not one to judge how a woman uses her body, but I won't deny I'm feeling a little out of place.

This is how Linc spends his free time—partying with women who are willing to give him anything he wants without any attachment.

The room is wall to wall with people dancing, mostly the girls with each other or on the laps of bikers.

When a shrill laugh sounds from the other side of the bar, I look over and see Stacia hanging off Linc's arm, trying to be the center of his attention. To his credit, he doesn't seem at all interested in having her there, but it's making me wonder if this is why he didn't seem to want me and Lucy here tonight. He may look a little irritated having her there, but then why wouldn't he just shrug her off? And why the hell do I care?

Lucy asks what I want to drink, pulling my attention away from Linc and his "friend." The man behind the bar, wearing a patch that says prospect, plops down two beers in front of us, then immediately goes back to Linc and leans over the bar to tell him something. Linc and Stacia turn their gaze in our direction. The human barnacle has a sour look on her face when Linc detaches from her clutches and makes his way over to us.

"Decided to come join the party, Charlie Pie?"

Oh God, another nickname. While the last couple attempts were cute, this time nothing but annoyance prickles at me.

"Yup," I reply, popping the P.

Linc looks from me to Lucy, then back to me with confusion written across his face. Honestly, I'm a little confused by my reaction, too. I have no claim on him. He can flirt or fuck anyone he wants. It's obvious he's done both with Stacia.

"You still tired from the trip?" he asks, trying to start a conversation.

"Nope."

"Okay," he draws out, obviously still not getting that I don't want to talk to him.

Lucy chuckles and shakes her head, muttering "dumbass" under her breath.

I shoot her a glare, and she shrugs as though she can't possibly understand why I don't need her commentary at this moment.

"Did I do something to upset you," Linc asks. "I didn't think the nickname was that bad." Linc laughs at his own joke, and I continue to stare at my beer.

"Why would you think that?" I ask with an attitude that surprises even me. Unfortunately, I don't have the fucks to give.

Linc's head cocks to the side. "Well, you've barely looked at me since I walked over here," he replies, glancing back toward where he came from. As soon as his eyes land on Stacia, his confusion clears and is replaced with irritation.

"Look, Charlie, I'm not some knight in shining armor who's lived a chaste life. If that's what you're expecting, you've got the wrong guy."

"You think that's what I expect from you?" I shoot him a scathing glare. "I never thought you were some sort of sainted biker, for chrissake."

"Listen, I'm not going to tiptoe around you just because you're staying here for the time being. This isn't your life, but it is mine. I don't dig the jealousy angle, Charlie."

The nerve of this man.

"I never once told you to be anything you aren't. You're more than entitled to have your fun." I look around the clubhouse at everyone having a good time—dancing and drinking, and generally not giving a fuck about what anyone thinks. "In fact, I think I'll do the same."

I grab my beer and Lucy's hand and make my way to the pool tables.

Fishing a quarter out of my pocket, I slap it on the edge of the table. "I've got the next game," I tell the group of bikers.

Barrett is among them, and he looks from me to Linc. "Sounds good," he says, nodding his head.

Another wave of irritation comes over me. Did he seriously just do that man look thing with Linc to get his permission? I would look over to the biker in question, but if he can have fun without "tip-toeing," then so can I.

Lucy and I make our way to where the pool cues are hanging against the wall, each of us grabbing one and the blue cue chalk.

"Charlie, while I love this 'badass, no one is going to make me feel like I don't matter attitude' you got going on, do you remember how bad you are at pool? Like seriously, you're one of the worst I've ever seen."

She's completely right. I actually hate pool, probably because I suck so bad at it. The ridiculous fact that I'm more interested in making Linc jealous—for reasons I'm not going to touch—rather than being concerned with pissing off a 6'2" biker in his own clubhouse and probably causing myself public embarrassment is not lost on me. Too bad I'm past the point of caring.

It's all been too much, too fast. Seeing Linc again, having some weird and completely foreign feelings for a man I don't really know, then being carted to Massachusetts because my ex found me and shot up the bar I worked at has my common sense flying right out the window. But you know what? I'm so fucking tired of being scared all the time and always watching my back. That's going to change, at least for one night.

"This isn't about the game Lucy. It's about having fun." I shoot her a wide smile that she sees through in an instant.

"Oh, it's about a game alright." She arches her brow, looking at the group of bikers standing around the pool table. "Just not this one."

CHAPTER NINE
LINC

"**W**ell, this is going spectacularly well," Jude says from next to me as I watch Charlie chalk her pool stick and blow the dust off. It makes me wonder if the little vixen realizes the half-boner she's giving my brothers right now. Shit, the way her lips form that O when she blows is far from having no effect on me.

"She can do what she wants. I'm not going to stop her from letting loose for the night."

Jude barks out a laugh and shakes his head. "No, you're just going to sit here seething instead." He clasps a hand on my shoulder. "Great plan, mate."

The truth of the matter is, Charlie can do whatever she wants with whoever she wants. I told her that was how I lived my life, after all. I certainly can't expect her not to do the same, and yet... I swipe a hand over my face. Jesus, what the hell has gotten into me?

Part of me is glad she saw Stacia hanging on me. Charlie doesn't need any ideas in her head that I'm anything more than a guy who likes to ride bikes with his brothers and is wholly averse to having any sort of long-term attachments. That's the last thing I need in my life. I'd already been sent away for six years, and there's always a chance a man who lives the life I do could do a lot more time. There's no way in hell I would want to leave my woman to deal with the fallout from that. I can't promise anyone anything more than a couple rolls between my sheets. It's for their own good as much as mine. And yet...

"I need another beer," I say to my friend, signaling to the prospect behind the bar.

"Sounds good. Let's drown our worries tonight. We can unpack all this shit tomorrow," Jude says, holding up his own bottle.

"There's nothing to unpack."

"No? My mistake," he says, raising his fresh beer to his lips. "Damn, I didn't realize all that was under those loose jeans she was wearing the other night."

I look toward where Jude has his eyes fixed and watch as Charlie bends over the pool table, her ass practically hanging out of the tight shorts she's wearing. When I look at my brothers, it's obvious I'm not the only one noticing. It's ridiculous that in a room full of half-naked women, my brothers can't stop staring at the girl who has the most skin covered.

I'd like to say it doesn't bother me in the least, but I've never been very good at lying to myself, and Jude sees through my bullshit, anyway.

"You may want to go over there and give her some tips on making the ball in the pocket before someone else does, if you catch my drift."

I look at my best friend and the urge to punch him in the face is strong.

"You one of the guys who would like to coach her on that?" I snarl through clenched teeth.

Jude looks at me and chuckles. "Nope. I'm not one to encroach on another man's territory."

"She's not my anything. Just someone who was dealt a shit hand, and I'm trying to help."

Jude laughs again, and I'm finding it harder and harder to see what he thinks is so damn funny.

"Whatever you say, mate."

Stacia saunters over with a couple shots in her hand as Charlie rounds to the other side of the table and studies the balls.

"I got us a couple shots, baby. If you want, we can grab a bottle and head back to your room," she purrs, handing me the small glass.

That's exactly what I should do. I should take Stacia back to my room and fuck her all night. Unfortunately for both of us, the idea turns sour in my stomach the moment I consider it.

I grab the shot from Stacia's hand and down it without waiting for her to drink hers.

"Not tonight, Stac."

She gives me an annoying pout and looks over to where I just had my gaze set. "I see," she says glaring at Charlie. "Well, you know where to find me if you change your mind."

Stacia has always been a nice girl, but it hasn't escaped my attention that she's been a little clingy lately. I've never made any promises to her about things being more than what they are. She's seen me with other girls, shit she's been in my bed with me and other girls, but lately, something has changed. Now with Charlie here, she seems to be trying even harder to insert herself.

I hear a cheer come from the pool tables and see my brother, Barrett, grabbing Charlie by the waist and swinging her around.

I see red.

Before I know what I'm doing, my feet are carrying me to the pool table, where I stand with my legs spread apart and my arms crossed over my chest right behind Charlie and Barrett.

"What's so exciting over here?" I ask with gritted teeth as Barrett and Charlie look at me over her shoulder.

"This pool shark just made the winning shot," Barrett replies.

"Why are you happy about it?" I ask. "You weren't on the same team."

Barrett sets Charlie down with a sheepish look as Charlie's eyes shoot fire in my direction.

"He can't be happy I finally made a shot?" she asks, jutting her hip out and resting her fist on it.

"He can and obviously is, considering he felt the need to manhandle you to celebrate, even though you beat him."

"I don't mind losing to a pretty girl," Barrett says with a laugh, attempting to defuse the situation. Apparently, my brother has no sense of self-preservation.

"Why do you care so much?" Charlie asks. "You're more than welcome to go back over there with Stacia," she says, pointing to where I just came from. "And do more shots with your club bunny."

Barrett finally wises up and takes a step back while Charlie and I move toward each other until we're almost toe to toe.

"I thought we already established that I'm not going to tiptoe around you?"

"And neither am I," Charlie responds.

Jude walks up next to me, watching the scene unfold.

"Charlie, why don't you and Lucy go back to your room? It's been a long couple days, and I'm sure you girls need the rest."

"Why should she have to go back anywhere, Jude? She's a grown-ass woman who can make her own decisions," Lucy says after putting her cue stick on the wall.

"Listen Lucifer, tensions are high right now, and I'm just asking everyone to go back to their corners and chill the fuck out."

"Really? Because it seems to me you're only talking to Charlie," Lucy replies, back straight and arms crossed.

"You know what? I think I will go back to my room," Charlie says. "I've seen all I needed to." Turning on her heel, she walks back toward the hallway leading to the bedrooms.

Well, fuck that if she thinks she gets the last word.

She's halfway to her room when I catch up to her and take her by the elbow, spinning her to face me. I realize too late what I've done or how this could affect her, considering her past, but she doesn't look scared at all when she turns toward me. No, she looks ready for a fight.

"What was that all about out there? Are you trying to make me jealous?" Being this close to her without all the noise from the party in the other room, I hear her panting breath and feel the energy radiating off her. She backs up against the wall, but it's not fear in her eyes. It's something entirely different. Something I've fantasized about too many times.

"You don't need to manhandle me, Linc," she says, her breath coming faster when she puts her hand on my chest. She probably means to push me away, but instead, her palm rests there, feeling my chest rise and fall with my own breaths.

"Why do you make me feel this way?" The question slips out without me meaning to voice it aloud. I've asked myself over and over why this girl has me wanting to be everything for her, to be the knight in shining armor I told her I wasn't.

"I'm not doing anything. You followed me, remember?"

"I do. The question I have is why. I've never once before cared if a woman stomped away with a fucking bee up her ass. Why is it different with you?"

"I don't know," she whispers, her gaze focused on my lips.

My hand moves from her elbow and skates up her arm, then over her shoulder to cup the side of her neck. Her pulse is hammering as my thumb grazes along her jaw to her pouty pink lip. They aren't caked with lipstick or sticky gloss but are smooth and full under my thumb. Charlie's heavy-lidded eyes are full of fire. Not the angry fire from earlier, but the kind that could get us both into a mess of trouble if we allow it to burn. And goddamn, at this moment, I'd gladly let it.

"I don't think I can give you what you want, what you deserve."

"You don't know what I want," she rushes out, her gaze never leaving mine. "What do you think I want?"

"I think you want me to taste your lips as much as I've been dying to." I lean my head closer, so close I can feel the pant of her breaths against my mouth.

A throat clears from the end of the hallway, and Charlie jumps in my hold. I drop my hand from her neck, disappointment ricocheting through me. We turn and see Lucy standing there with a knowing smile.

"Am I interrupting something?"

"Yes," I answer at the same time Charlie tells her friend no.

Charlie slides away from me and my other hand, which was caressing the sliver of soft skin between the bottom of her shirt and the top of her sexy-as-hell shorts.

"Sorry about being kind of a bitch earlier." Charlie's eyes meet mine briefly, then dart to the floor. I have a feeling I know what she's going to say next. "I think Jude's right. It's been a long couple of days, and I need a good night's sleep." Dammit, I was really hoping to be wrong.

"Please don't say that loud enough for him to hear," Lucy scoffs as she walks toward us. "The man is insufferable as it is."

Though my eyes don't leave Charlie's, her gaze is anywhere but on me.

"Charlie," I say, reaching out and clasping her hand before she walks away. I have no idea what I want to say, but I want her to look at me one more time. "Goodnight."

"Goodnight, Linc," she says, giving me her eyes one more time, then turns toward her room.

I don't know if anything would have gone further than a simple kiss. Scratch that. It would have gone a lot further, but Lucy interrupting was probably for the best. There's still too much unknown about everything that's going on, and until it gets sorted, best not to blur the lines.

The annoying voice in the back of my mind is whispering too late.

"Linc, I need a word," Ozzy calls the next morning as I'm grabbing a coffee from the kitchen. I slept like shit last night. The heat from the soft skin of Charlie's neck was burned into my palm and the way her eyes were wide and filled with lust seared into my brain.

"Be right there."

Since he didn't call church, I'm assuming he means for me to meet him in his office. When I get there, he's behind his desk with his fingers steepled under his chin.

"Got a call from the Italians this morning," he tells me.

"What do those fucks want?"

To say we don't have the best relationship with those assholes is putting it mildly. Since they shot up our clubhouse when Ozzy, Knox, and I were in high school and Trick, who was president at the time, put a bunch of their capos to ground for the attack, tensions have never been anything but high.

"Seems Charlie's ex got a hold of a capo through one of his dealers. Said there was some info his ex had on the Irish and us, and he offered to sell it to them."

"Wait, his cousin is part of the Irish crew we deal guns with, and he's reaching out to their rival organization to sell out his blood?" I sit back in my chair and shake my head. Can't say I'm surprised. Just goes to show what a complete waste of life that scumbag is.

"Why were they calling you?"

"The ex told them we have Charlie here. Said if they want the info, then he wants the Italians to provide backup when he comes to get her. Apparently, the two guys who were in Texas with him didn't know she was protected by the club. They tucked tail and ran, but Jace is still out for blood."

"The only blood that's going to be spilled is that dumbfuck's." I stew in anger for a moment before speaking again. "Why did they call you to give you a heads-up?"

"They wanted to make a deal. I suppose they figured since it's apparently widespread knowledge that she's hiding something, they thought we'd want her taken off our hands."

"The fuck we do," I blurt out.

Ozzy holds up his hands in a placating gesture.

"Don't worry. I told them I have no idea who Charlie is. The last thing we need is the Italians storming the castle." Ozzy tilts his head, studying me. "Is there something going on between the two of you?"

I'm not sure how to answer that. I'm not about to lie to my president after everything he's done for me... and for Charlie.

"Honestly, Oz, I don't know where my head's at right now. There's something about her I can't walk away from. I don't want to, even if I could."

"You're talking like you want to make her your old lady."

"Woah. Let's not get ahead of ourselves. I'm a long way off from giving her my patch. Shit, I haven't even kissed her yet."

Ozzy smirks. "Is your famous charm finally going cold?"

"Fuck off," I laugh out, and Ozzy chuckles.

"I called the Irish to give them a heads-up. Since the Italians are trying to make a deal, I wanted to make sure they were aware and let them know they have a turncoat. Spoke to Finnegan. They had no idea Cillian's cousin went after you in Texas. Jace isn't connected himself, just Cillian. And they are none too happy about Jace or the shootout in Texas, let alone the bomb I dropped on them." Ozzy leans further back in his chair, looking me directly in the eye.

"They know Charlie has some information and want assurances she doesn't plan to use anything against them." He scrubs a hand over his face. "Shit, I'd like the same. If you don't plan on making her your old lady,"—I open my mouth to protest, but he holds a hand in the air to stop me—"I'm not saying you need to, but if that's not your plan, I'd feel a hell of a lot better about having whatever she has in my possession."

I nod in agreement. "Fair."

"I told Finnegan we would handle it."

I really hope he's not saying what I think he's saying as I eye him suspiciously.

"Get that look off your goddamn face, Linc. You know damn well I would never lay a finger on a woman."

Fuck, of course, I know that. This intense urge to protect Charlie from any harm is seriously fucking with my head.

"What I meant is I know you'll figure out where and what this information is and what she was planning on doing with it. I don't want her deciding to turn state's evidence against Jace to get him off her back or some shit. Not if it means we get caught in the crossfire."

"I'll figure it out, Prez."

Ozzy nods once more and looks at the mountain of paperwork on his desk. "Keep me updated," he replies before muttering to himself about how much he hates all this damn paperwork.

I stand from my chair, and as I reach the door, Ozzy calls out to me.

"You know we have your back and Charlie's and her friend's by extension, yeah?"

"I know."

"Alright," Ozzy replies, waving his hand for me to leave.

I go back to the kitchen and grab another cup of coffee. Fuck, this just keeps getting more and more complicated.

There's one thing I know for sure. It's no use denying that whether or not I like it, Charlie is mine to protect. What it means beyond that is anyone's guess. The Italians and the Irish will definitely think twice about trying to take what's mine. They'll have to go through me and my brothers to get to her now.

But first things first. I want to make sure Charlie can defend herself if she ever needs to.

Jude walks into the kitchen as I'm mulling over the new shitstorm we've found ourselves in.

"Hey, man, fancy some target practice?"

Jude's smile is wider than I would expect for this time in the morning, but there's nothing like blowing off some steam at the range.

"Let's do it, mate."

CHAPTER TEN
CHARLIE

"Have you ever shot a gun before Cha Cha?" Linc asks with a laugh. "Okay, that one was horrible when I said it out loud."

"Gee, ya think?" Lucy asks from beside me in an open field, where there are various targets set up for my first shooting lesson.

"Yeah, what is with the terrible nicknames?" Jude asks while inspecting the array of guns he has laid out on the table next to us.

"Who doesn't love a good nickname?" Linc says.

I raise my hand. "Me. I don't love nicknames. Not to mention not a single one has been good."

"It's a work in progress. Don't worry, Charlie cake, I'll find one." The teasing smile on his face is giving me those gooey feelings on the inside, even if the nicknames aren't.

When Lucy and I emerged from our room this morning, Linc informed me that he wanted to see how well I handled a gun. I promptly informed him I never had, so it would be a surprise for both of us. If I was worried things would feel weird after our almost kiss last night, I shouldn't have been. He's acting like it never happened. Now, I'm worried about why he's so unaffected. My mind is seriously a fucked-up place to be today.

"Okay, let's go through the moving parts here," Linc says before showing me the different weapons. He goes over each one on the table, explaining how to load and reload clips, the safety, and making sure to explain the only time you have your finger on the trigger is when you're ready to fire. He shows me how to stand and breathe while I shoot and where to shoot if, heaven forbid, I ever have to defend myself.

"Don't aim for the head. It's a smaller target. Aim for the chest. You have a better chance of hitting something," he says, standing behind me as I practice aiming at one of those paper target things.

"Can I ask you a question?" I lower my gun to the ground, making sure the safety is on before turning to him.

"Sure."

"What do you think the chances are that I'm going to need to use this?" I ask, looking down at my hand.

"Honestly?" Linc takes a breath in and lets it out slowly. "I'd love nothing more than to tell you this is just a precautionary measure, but with the shit going on and your ex, who is obviously not afraid to open fire, I'd say they're enough that I want to make sure you're comfortable handling a firearm."

I nod, appreciating his honesty.

"Listen, babe," he says, taking the gun from my hand and setting it next to the others. "I will do everything in my power to make sure it never comes to it, but this is for your own peace of mind as much as mine."

Linc tucks a lock of hair that's fallen from my ponytail behind my ear. His hand cups the side of my neck as he brushes his thumb against the line of my jaw—just like he did last night. And just like last night, I feel my heart thumping wildly in my chest from his touch.

"Are we flirting or shooting," Jude calls from a few feet away.

Letting out an embarrassed giggle, I step away from Linc and pick up the weapon, checking the clip and safety like he showed me.

"Alright. Let's do some target practice." Linc comes up behind me and presses into my back, adjusting my stance.

God, the man smells so good. There's no lingering smoke or booze smell from last night, just that freshly showered, clean smell.

"You're distracting me," I say out of the side of my mouth so no one else overhears.

"Good," he says, turning his head slightly to bury his nose in my hair, inhaling deeply. He straightens and moves back a full step. "There's going to be a lot more distracting you if you're ever in a position to have to use that thing."

Dick.

"Okay, now remember what I said about not locking your elbows and taking slow and steady breaths."

I nod once.

"Go for it."

I squeeze the trigger, and the kickback is stronger than I expect. Peering at the target, I see I didn't even come close to hitting it.

"Don't worry about being perfect your first time out. This is about getting used to the feel of it in your hand."

I dip my chin, trying to fight the disappointment.

"Try again."

Focusing back on the target, I line up my shot and pop off three more rounds.

"You're getting better, but you're tensing too much before you fire. Breathe out slowly as you squeeze," Lucy coaches from beside me.

"I didn't realize we had an expert in our midst," Jude comments. "Why don't you let Linc teach her since he's the one with experience."

Lucy swings her gaze to Jude, and a small smile creeps across her mouth.

Uh-oh. I know that smile.

Lucy saunters over to the table with the guns and glides her fingers over the selection. She settles on a handgun that looks way bigger than anything I would be comfortable holding and strides over to Jude. She turns to the target he has set up for himself and lifts the pistol, popping off three quick shots. When she lowers her arm, she looks at Jude with a wide smile. He looks toward the target with two holes in the chest and one in the head.

"You were saying?" she asks with a scowl when he looks back at her.

"Seems we have a ringer over here," he calls to Linc. "Where did you learn to shoot like that?" Jude is looking at Lucy, suspicion swirling in his gaze.

"There's a lot you don't know about me, biker boy, and you never will."

Walking back over to the chair she was watching from, she picks up the magazine she was reading, crosses her legs, and sits tall.

Jude is speechless as he watches her with a discerning gaze. He doesn't know what to make of my raven-haired best friend, and I can tell it's not sitting well with him.

"Did you know she had that kind of aim?" Linc asks me.

"I didn't even know she'd ever held a gun." I have a feeling this has something to do with the past she doesn't like to talk about. It makes me wonder if she'll ever be comfortable opening up to me. The idea sends a small pang of sadness through my chest when I think about what my best friend must have been through.

"I have to admit," Linc starts, "I feel a little ill-equipped to teach you now. It looks like Lucy has me beat on the skills level."

We both look at Lucy as she turns the page of her magazine, pretending not to hear a word we're saying.

The satisfied smile on her face tells me she heard him loud and clear.

I turn to Linc. "You're doing just fine," I reassure. "Besides, I don't think she likes guns very much."

"Could have fooled me." Linc looks back to the targets. "Let's keep practicing."

Two hours later, I'd shot every one of the guns they had out for us. I can't say I'm much better than when I started, but I'm definitely more comfortable. And I did manage to hit the target a couple times. Not the actual body printed on it, just the white paper around it.

The afternoon passes with Lucy and me hanging out in our room and Linc and Jude doing whatever it is bikers do. My stomach growls around dinner time, so Lucy and I decide now's a good time to head to the kitchen to scrounge up some food. I know the bunnies do most of the cooking around here, but there's something about eating the food they make that doesn't sit right with me. It's apparent from Stacia and a couple of the other girls, they aren't exactly thrilled with us being here. Even though they've been anything but welcoming, I don't want to feel like I'm taking advantage.

When we enter the kitchen, there's an older woman at the oven taking out a dish that smells absolutely heavenly. She looks over to me standing in the doorway, and I contemplate whether we should stay or leave. I've never seen her before, but the last thing I want to deal with is more attitude.

"Hi there. You must be Charlie and Lucy," she greets, setting the pan on top of the stove and removing the flowery oven mitts. She reaches out to shake my hand. "I'm Tanya. Linc and Knox's mom."

Relief, followed swiftly by embarrassment, runs through me. I can't believe I thought Linc's mom was a bunny.

"Hi, nice to meet you," I reply, shaking her hand before Lucy does the same. Then guilt hits me. This woman lost her son for six years because of me. I brace myself, waiting for her to bring it up like Jude did, but she does the opposite. She leans in for a hug.

"Linc told me your situation way back when he went to prison. I'm so glad my son was able to help back then, and I'm thankful he's able to be here for you now. There's nothing worse than thinking you have nowhere and no one to turn to when you're in that situation."

The tone in her voice tells me she's lived it, too. I want to ask more—like how do you ever trust someone not to hurt you again or how can she not hate me for being part of the reason her son went to prison—but I settle for her warm embrace instead.

"Now," Tanya says, breaking the hug. "Would you ladies mind helping me out with getting all this into the dining room? Those bunnies seem to make themselves scarce whenever I come around."

"Probably because the last time you were around one, she tried to sit in Trick's lap, and you almost pulled her out of the clubhouse by her extensions," Linc says, coming into the kitchen.

"Oh please, that was years ago," Tanya says, waving her hand.

"What can I say, Mom? Your reputation precedes you." Linc walks up to his mom and gives her a huge bear hug, lifting her off her feet.

"Put me down, you brute, and help your mother. I made you boys' favorite, meatloaf with all the fixings."

He sets her on her feet, gives her a loud kiss on the cheek, and turns around to inspect the pan.

"Sometimes you just have to show these women who's boss, right?" Tanya asks, giving me a conspiratorial wink.

How do I tell this woman the only man I've ever been slightly possessive over is her son, who I barely know and have no right feeling that way about? The only other relationship I was in was with Jace, and there was no way I would ever care if another woman flirted with him. If she wanted him, the only thing I would have told her was she could do better. Hell, I could have done better myself, but there was no one around to warn me back then.

Instead of word vomiting all over Linc's mom, I give her a small smile of agreement.

Thoughts swirl in my head. What would it be like to be in a relationship with someone you actually wanted to lay claim to in front of everyone? The urge certainly wasn't there with my ex, but he always made sure everyone knew I was his. Not because he loved me or cherished me, but more like I was his property, and he wanted to make sure everyone was aware. There were no soft touches or lingering smiles. It was all about exerting his control in front of everyone.

The idea that I would be in a position to do something like Tanya did and not get slapped or kicked for overstepping is completely foreign to me. The desire to want to is even more so. But if Linc and I were together, I wonder if he would have a problem with it. Last night, he didn't seem to like the idea of being tied to one woman or feeling the need to answer to anyone. He also didn't like anyone else flirting with me or vice versa. It's all so confusing.

I look over at the man in question and smile at the way he's inhaling the scent of the meatloaf. The groan that reverberates deep from his throat makes me laugh.

"For the love of everything holy, son, could you not make those noises while you stare at the food like it's your last meal?" his mom chastises. "You're liable to scare poor Charlie over here."

"I don't think Charlie minds my groans, do you, Charlie cat?" he replies with a wink.

"The groans, I don't mind. The nicknames, on the other hand..."

Linc's mom watches her son with a keen eye while I try not to blush furiously over the sounds that just came from him.

"You love them," he tells me.

"You know what I would love more?" I arch my brow. "To eat."

Linc lets out a full belly laugh as I grab the giant bowl of mashed potatoes.

"Now, here's a girl who loves her meat."

I walk past him and shoot him a teasing glare. "Idiot."

Dinner is a loud and frenzied affair as every biker in the compound comes out of the woodwork when they hear Tanya made dinner. I watch in awe as they demolish the trays of meatloaf, veggies, and potatoes.

"Jesus." I take in the scene in front of me. "It's like we're in a room full of teenage wrestlers trying to go up a weight class."

"Oh, honey, this is the norm around here. You should have seen the amount of food I had to cook just to feed Knox, Linc, and Ozzy growing up. Between the three of them, there wouldn't be a pan that wasn't practically licked clean." She smiles at the sight of everyone enjoying her food. Knox comes over and gives her a sweet kiss on the cheek.

"Thanks, Mom. You didn't have to do this." He looks around the room. "Where's Trick tonight?"

"Annual camping trip with Gramps."

Knox nods his head and goes to sit with Ozzy and a couple of the other guys I've seen around but haven't spent much time with.

"Who's Trick?" I ask, wondering how everyone knows him, but I've yet to meet anyone by that name.

"My old man and Ozzy's dad. He used to be president and Gramps before him."

"Are you Ozzy's mom, too?"

They all refer to each other as brother, so I have no idea who's actually related to whom.

"No, honey, I didn't meet Trick and the club until my boys were older. We moved here from Nebraska. I left a situation that was similar to yours," she says, reaching over to squeeze my hand. "And I never looked back. I met Trick's mom when I came into their bike shop to see if they needed help at the front desk. Janine, Trick's mom, was just about at the end of her rope trying to keep these guys organized and hired me on the spot." She has a warm smile on her face, the memory obviously one she cherishes. "Anyway," she says, shaking her head, "that's how I met the club, and a few years later, I figured I would give Trick a shot. The rest is history."

Tanya looks around the room like an adoring mom would look at her family, then sets her sights back on me.

"I wish I didn't have to go through what I went through back in Nebraska, but if that's what it took to get me here, then I know I ended up exactly where I was meant to be. When I stopped being scared that every man was like my ex, I was finally able to see there were good men in the world."

"Trick is a good man?"

"The best. They all are, really. Trick would never run a club that stood by when women were being hurt. None of these boys would, either. He showed Linc and Knox what it meant to be good men, too. I wish there were more like them."

Linc sits down next to me and digs into his plate. I wonder what it would be like to have this be my normal. To have dinner with this man every night in a room full of people who care about each other. What it would be like to have a woman in my life who took the time out of her day to feed the people she loves and look so damn happy doing it. What if one of these days, it was me cooking and part of this huge extended family?

I always thought it wasn't in the cards for me, that it would just be me and Lucy, but I'm starting to think having more sounds like a damn good idea. Not that I'm in any position to make that decision now, not with everything hanging over our heads, but when we're on the other side of this, who knows? Maybe finally feeling like I can settle in one place without looking over my shoulder all the time could actually happen.

Tanya hollers at Ozzy to get some of the girls to clean. She did the cooking. The least they can do is the cleaning.

"Yes, ma'am," he calls back and stands.

Never in my life would I have imagined the burly MC president would take orders from someone, especially a woman, but if what Tanya said was true, they hold women in the highest regard. I have a feeling if they didn't, Tanya would have no problem making sure they didn't make that mistake twice.

When dinner ends and the bunnies have cleaned the mess, Tanya makes her exit, giving me an extra-long hug.

"You call me if you need help with anything, honey. My door is always open to you."

For some reason, hearing that makes me want to cry. The realization that someone who went through years of abuse can have a full life and not be scared of her own shadow wasn't something I thought possible for myself. Tanya is proof to the contrary.

Lucy and I decide to play some pool, neither of us ready to go back to our room. When Linc sees me racking up the balls, he comes over and grabs a stick.

"Let's play teams. Me and you against Lucy and Jude."

"Lucifer and I are hardly a good match, mate," Jude says, side-eyeing Lucy.

"Are you still butt hurt I kicked your ass at the range today?"

"First of all," he says, holding up a finger, "you only fired three shots. There was no ass-kicking when you haven't proven you can do that more than once. And second,"—he holds up another finger—"the only butt that's going to be hurting is going to be yours when I bend you over my knee and spank your ass red."

A furious blush covers Lucy's face as she turns to grab a cue for herself.

Huh, that's curious.

We play a few games, Linc giving me pointers on how to better set up a shot. Jude and Lucy are at least tolerating each other, keeping the barbs and dirty looks to a minimum. When Linc decides my stance and the way I hold my arms needs work, he moves behind me and leans over me to "help" me adjust the way I'm holding the cue.

"I'm beginning to think the only reason you wanted me to play was so you could cop a cheap feel."

His chuckle vibrates into my body from behind. "Who me? I thought you wanted to get better at pool."

His warm breath tickles the side of my face when he speaks in a low voice, making my body feel like it's about to combust. Never in my life would I have thought the feel of someone's breath against my face would have me wanting to toss the stick down and throw myself at him in a room full of people.

When I take the shot, the ball goes into the hole.

"See, you just needed a little adjustment," he comments before standing upright.

That's not all I need right now.

Of course, Jude and Lucy still win, and Linc hands him a twenty.

"Pleasure doing business with you," Jude tells him.

It's getting late, and I can tell Lucy is tired but doesn't want to leave me alone.

"Hey, we're going to head to bed," I tell Linc. "Thanks for the gun and pool lessons.

"Any time, Charlie girl." He smiles wide and takes the cue from my hand.

"Again... not a dog."

Linc grabs me around the waist and brings me flush to his chest before growling in my ear. "No, but I wouldn't mind petting you just the same."

Holy shit, I've never wanted to be a Labrador Retriever more in my damn life.

"Sweet dreams." He releases me and shoots me a wink.

My breath stalls in my chest as a shiver of excitement runs down my spine, then I hear Lucy let out a loud yawn across the table.

"Night," I squeak out before grabbing Lucy's hand and hauling her to our bedroom.

"Okay. You need to tell me what the hell is going on with you two," Lucy says as I grab my pajamas and head to the bathroom to get ready for bed.

"Fuck if I know. He's flirty, that's for damn sure."

"Girl, when he growled in your ear, *my* panties almost went up in flames, and I was a solid six feet from you two."

I laugh, but she isn't wrong. Linc is a man built for pleasure, and that sexy growl thing he does could melt a fucking glacier.

I come out of the bathroom and sit on the other bed, facing my best friend.

"I haven't been with anyone since Jace," I confess.

Lucy looks at me with a sad understanding in her eyes.

"I figured," she says in a thoughtful tone. "But, honey, that man looks like he could make you scream in soprano, if you know what I mean, which is a lot more than anyone would ever say about your ex. To top it off, he's practically salivating over the chance for you to let him." Lucy turns off the light on the nightstand and climbs under the covers. "And if I were you, I would give him a chance."

"Maybe." She has some good points. I think about the day we spent together and the kiss that almost was last night. There was a strength in holding that gun earlier, and Linc caring about me being prepared to defend myself was so fucking sexy. No one other than Lucy ever cared about my personal safety. Seeing the way he and the rest of the club treated his mom was icing on the cake. So many check marks are making their way into the yes column. It makes me wonder what would happen if I threw caution to the wind for the night and knocked on the biker's door.

Though I'm not a virgin, I've never been with a man who really knows what he's doing in bed. With Jace, it was more of a let's get this over with kind of situation. When he was done, it was lights out. Linc, though? Linc strikes me as the kind of man who wouldn't dream of letting a woman out of his bed without showing her what lies on the other side of heaven. I may not have a strong belief in God, but something tells me he'd have me calling out to him several times before the night was through.

CHAPTER ELEVEN
LINC

I watch Charlie as she and Lucy head back to their room for the night. Having her here and meeting my mom, completely unexpectedly, is turning out to be a lot more than I bargained for. Before leaving, my mom pulled me aside.

"She's a good girl, Linc, but she has demons. If you're going to do nothing but mess around with her, then leave it be."

I let her know that I have no intention of going there with Charlie. That may have been the first time I lied to my mom, and the look in her eyes told me she knew I was full of shit.

"Spill," Jude commands when we're sitting at the bar after putting the pool cues away for the night.

"What are you talking about?"

I'm not an idiot. I know he saw the way I said good-night to Charlie. There are two reasons for that. The first is, last night, the only person who saw the almost kiss was Lucy. Since we aren't a bunch of gossiping fourteen-year-old girls, I hadn't told anyone about it, not even Jude. But every brother in the place tonight saw what I was doing. Charlie isn't a bunny, and I just pissed a circle around her. Second, I wanted to. That's it. I wanted to feel her pert little ass pressed against me when she was bending over the pool table, and I was pretending to try to help her. I wanted to feel the shiver I knew would come when I growled in her ear.

Last night, I was determined to keep her at a distance. Well, until the end of the night. I knew as soon as she melted into me when I was pressed close to her, she would be mine, and the idea of no strings attached would fly right out the damn window.

"I'm talking about the little scene you and Charlie put on. Are you planning on taking the little bird to bed then?" Jude asks with a knowing smile.

"What if I am?"

"Don't get your knickers in a twist. I like Charlie. She seems like a sweet girl. Just remember, there's a lot of heat attached to her."

I have no interest in rehashing this conversation with Jude again, and the glare I send him says exactly that.

"I can tell you want to haul off and hit me," he says with a smirk. "But I wouldn't be the asshole you know and love if I didn't at least remind you before you start thinking with your dick instead of your head."

"I can think with both just fine."

"That doesn't even make sense."

"Wanker." I shoot him another dirty look and throw up my middle finger for good measure.

"That's my word." Jude shakes his head. "It doesn't sound right with your stupid American accent."

"I don't have a stupid accent. You do."

"Fuck off." Jude throws a beer cap, hitting me in the side of the face.

Later that night as I'm lying in bed, I remember Charlie's soft gasp when I pressed into her. Fuck, that sound nearly had my cock punching through my jeans. Never in my life have I had such a primal reaction to a woman. When I picked her up on the side of the road all those years ago, the need to protect her was overwhelming. Back then, it didn't have anything to do with attraction or wanting her in my bed. How I feel about her now, though, is more complicated. There's just something about those blue eyes and her soft way that calls to a part of me I never thought I had.

The urge to sneak into Charlie's room and finish what we started last night is strong. Honestly, if she wasn't rooming with a woman who would no doubt break a lamp over my head before figuring out who was there, I would.

A quiet knock sounds at my door. It isn't one of the bunnies, considering there are no obnoxious giggles coming from the other side. I grab the jeans next to my bed and slide them over my hips, leaving the top button undone, and stride across my room.

Opening the door, the sight in front of me nearly knocks me over. Charlie is standing there in a little tank top and those sexy-as-hell sleep shorts that leave nothing to the imagination. She bites her lip, looking nervous as a kitten.

"Hey, I, um, couldn't sleep?"

Her nerves are fucking adorable.

"Are you asking or telling me, sweetheart?" I raise my arm and rest it against the door jamb, leaning toward her. Charlie takes an audible gulp.

She's so damn cute right now, it makes my chest ache... among other things.

"God, this was a terrible idea. Goodnight."

She moves to walk away, but I gently grab her arm to stop her.

"This is the best idea you've had all night. Get in here." Pulling her inside the room, I shut the door with my foot before gently pushing her against it.

When she looks at me with those bottomless blue eyes, there's desire and nerves shining in them. The desire I want to see more of. The nerves, on the other hand, I can do without.

"Tell me what's on your mind?" My tone is gentle, even if the urges inside me are anything but. The last thing I want is to scare her away.

Charlie worries her bottom lip between her teeth and shrugs. I pull the abused flesh from her teeth with my thumb and gently swipe it against her soft pout.

"If anyone is going to be biting any part of you, it's going to be me."

"God, when you say things like that to me, I feel it here." Her hand moves across her lower belly.

"Tell me more," I prod, running my nose across the column of her neck, inhaling her sweet scent as I go. "I want to hear all your thoughts," I whisper.

"You make my head fuzzy. I can barely think, let alone talk when I'm around you."

I rest my forehead against hers, our lips just a breath apart.

"I've never felt like this before," she admits.

"Like what?" I ask, running my hand over her hip.

"This desperate need to let go and do what feels right. To do whatever I want and to hell with the consequences."

"I love the sound of that, sweetheart, but I need your words. I don't want to overstep any boundaries with you, even accidentally."

"I want you, Linc."

"I can't promise it's going to be soft, baby." I rest my forehead against hers. "I've been dying to feel you."

"So have I," she breathes out.

Good enough for me.

Slamming my mouth into hers, I finally taste the sweetness I've been craving. Charlie throws her arms around my neck, pressing her soft curves away from the wall and into me. My hands travel from her hips, down her round ass, and to the backs of her supple thighs before hoisting her. She wraps her legs tightly around my waist, and her center rubs against the bulge in my jeans, eliciting a needy whimper from her.

Tuning around, I take three long strides to my bed, gently laying Charlie down. I stand to my full height and drink in the goddess laying in front of me. With her arms above her head, she's stretched before me like a platter for me, and me alone, to feast on.

"I don't know where to start with you," I say, looking at all the creamy soft skin on display.

"Anywhere you want."

"That's a dangerous invitation."

She looks me in the eye. "No, it's not... not with you."

The confidence and surety that rings in her voice settle in my bones. Charlie knows I would never hurt her. She's here to share herself with me and knows I would sooner cut off my own hand than abuse that privilege.

Settling over her, I take her mouth in a deep kiss. I don't think I'll ever get enough of the way she tastes. Exploring her mouth and the sounds I can pull from her with my kiss alone is my new favorite pastime.

With her legs tangled in mine, I trail open-mouthed kisses down the center of her throat to her collarbone. The sight of her pulse thumping wildly under her silky soft skin calls to me. I lay my lips over the spot, swirling my tongue over it before moving lower. When I reach the top of her tank top, I rise onto my knees and trail my fingertips from her hands still over her head, down her arms, and over her ribs, eliciting a breathy laugh.

"Ticklish?"

"A little."

I save that nugget of information in the back of my mind for later.

When my hands reach the bottom of her shirt, instead of ripping it off, I glide my fingers over the soft patch of skin above the waist of her shorts.

"I think this right here is my favorite part of you."

She looks at me with a curious expression.

"There's this anticipation when you tremble beneath my fingers when I touch you here." I look down and watch her stomach tense and relax with my touch. "The possibilities of where my fingers are going to go next is torture, isn't it?" I dip my finger into the waistband of her shorts. "I could take these off and make you come harder than you ever have in your life."

She grips the pillow next to her head and rolls her hips below me, trying to find purchase on something to relieve the ache I'm enjoying building inside her.

"Or,"—I glide my fingers to her tank top that rests just below her breasts—"I could take this off and play with those sweet nipples I see under there, just begging for my mouth."

"Linc," she says on a gasp. "Yes, please. Any of it. All of it. Just stop torturing me."

I chuckle darkly. "If you insist."

Rising, I grab her shorts and swiftly tug them down her legs.

"Sweet Jesus, no panties. Naughty girl." I wink and lower myself to the bed, spreading her legs wide before I settle between her soft thighs. My finger runs the length of her wet center, and she arches into my touch. "Is this for me?" I ask, parting her lips slightly and brushing over her swollen nub.

"Yes," she moans.

"Then I'm going to lick what's mine."

Lowering my head to her pussy, I take my first taste of Charlie. Fuck, I have never in my life tasted something so goddamn delicious. My lips wrap around her clit, and I move my tongue ferociously over it. Charlie is writing on the bed, her hands tangling in my hair.

"Stay still so I can eat this sweet pussy."

She lets out a long groan but stops moving.

"That's my girl. Don't worry, I'll get you there."

I insert one finger into her tight channel. If the way her walls grip my finger is any indication, she's going to strangle my cock when I finally slide inside her.

"Oh, shit," she cries out when I turn my finger and find that spot inside to make her see stars.

Her legs clamp around my ears, muffling the loud moan that escapes while her walls strangle my finger as she comes completely undone. I remove the digit and continue to lick her, following her as she comes down from her orgasm. When her fingers loosen their tight grip in my hair, I look into the most beautiful, sated eyes I've ever seen. Her blissed-out smile has me wanting to pound my chest with male pride. Instead, I kiss my way up her stomach to her mouth. She opens and tastes herself on my tongue.

"Do you like tasting yourself?"

"I like tasting us together," she says before claiming my lips in another bruising kiss.

This isn't about her trying to do or say the things she thinks are sexy but are actually hollow. This is her letting go and giving into the pleasure she's never felt before. Doubt and uncertainty no longer have a place between us in my bed.

"I think it's time for me to give those nipples some attention," I tell her as I pull the bottom of her tank up and over her head. Taking a breath, because this is sensory overload of the best kind, I let my eyes feast on Charlie's naked body below me. Her tits are fucking perfect, with dusty-rose nipples that are in hardened points waiting for my mouth. Bending down, I circle my tongue around the bud, then suck it into my mouth.

"Fuck, you're goddamned perfect," I groan when I lift my head to bestow her other breast with the same attention.

"That feels so good, Linc. I need more." Charlie is a writhing mess of want under me, and I fucking love it.

"What do you need, baby?" Lifting my head, I stare into her bright eyes as I draw her nipple into my mouth and release it with a pop.

She bites her lip, shyness suddenly clouding her eyes.

"Hey, now, none of that. You can tell me anything you want, and I will do my damndest to give it to you. This is about you, Charlie, your pleasure. I'm just the lucky bastard that gets to give it to you."

"I want you inside me. I need you to fuck me." Her hands trail down my back before grabbing my ass and squeezing. My girl wants to play.

A wicked grin spreads across my face.

"It would be my pleasure."

Standing from the bed, I drop my jeans to the floor. Charlie takes a long look at my naked body as she rubs her thighs together in anticipation.

"Come here, baby."

She sits up on the bed and kneels in front of me. Grabbing her thighs, I wrap her legs around me and twist us around, falling back on the mattress with her straddling me. I reach over and grab a condom from my nightstand, rolling it on, then raising my hand to cup her neck.

"I want you to ride me. Use me however you need to make yourself come again."

With my hands on her hips, she lifts up and slowly lowers onto me, letting out a whoosh of breath when she's fully seated. I swear to fucking God, the clubhouse could catch fire right now and I wouldn't notice. The only thing I can think, feel, or taste is wrapped up in this perfect package.

Charlie slowly begins to move up and down, then once she finds a rhythm that suits her, she quickens her movements. With her face tilted toward the ceiling and her long, dark locks tickling my thighs, I'm about to blow inside of the most perfect pussy I've ever felt.

"Fuck, baby, that feels so good. Ride me just like that," I grit out.

"I need more," she says, sweat beading along her brow.

Moving one hand from her hip, I bring it around to rub her clit while she rides me.

"Yes, that's it. Oh, fuck," she draws out as her pussy clamps hard around me, setting off my own orgasm.

"Ahh," I cry out, falling into oblivion as I fill the condom.

Charlie collapses onto my sweaty chest, both of us panting like we just ran a goddamn marathon.

"That was..." She starts but can't seem to find the words to finish her sentence.

"Yeah," I breathe out.

There simply are no words to describe the utter rightness. I'm not a man to wax poetic about sex, but calling this anything other than life altering would be a lie. A shift took place in my chest, as though something moved to make room for something bigger than anything I've ever felt.

Charlie gingerly rises off me and collapses on the bed before I get up to take care of the condom. When I return to the bedroom, she's right where I left her and only semi-conscious.

"I should go back to my room. Lucy might wonder where I am if she wakes up."

"Or you could stay here. I have a feeling if Lucy wakes up, she'll know exactly where you are."

"True." Charlie lets out a sweet but tired giggle. "I think she knew this was going to happen before I did."

"She's a smart girl, that one." Charlie hums in agreement. "Let me rest for a minute." Lying back down, I pull her close to me and rub my face in her tousled hair. "Then I'll give those perfect tits more of the attention they deserve."

Charlie giggles again. God, I love that fucking sound.

"I think you gave every part of me the perfect amount of attention."

I pull my head back and lock my eyes with hers.

"Sweetheart, if you think the night's over, I hate to be the one to tell you that you're wrong. I'm just getting started with you."

CHAPTER TWELVE
LINC

Needless to say, Charlie and I got minimal sleep last night. Every time I opened my eyes from dozing off, I couldn't resist touching her. Those touches would wake her and soon turn into me being buried inside her tight heat once more.

Every time last night with Charlie blew my fucking mind. The longer the night went on, the more vocal she became about what she wanted and how she wanted it. The timid girl I've been trying to protect disappeared last night in my bed to be replaced with a woman with a sexual appetite that matched mine. And thank fuck for that. I wasn't about to bring it up last night, but I have a feeling Charlie hasn't been with many guys, and she sure as shit has never been with one who got off on a woman directing the show.

Shit, I'm not sure I've ever been that guy, to be honest. With any other girl, it was about me getting off. Sure, I always made sure they came, too, I'm not a total asshole, but I was always the one in control, and they seemed perfectly fine to let me take the lead. Or maybe

I just didn't care enough to give them the opportunity for something different.

Not with the girl lying next to me, cuddled into my chest. It was all about her and finding what she liked, and I thank my lucky fucking stars I get to be the man she explores that side of herself with.

My phone vibrates on the nightstand next to me, and I carefully move so I don't wake Charlie.

Oz: *Need to talk.*

Looking at Charlie's sleeping form next to me, I think about how long I can put him off. Considering this is Ozzy, I know it's not much.

Me: *Ok, give me 30.*

Ozzy doesn't respond, so I assume he has no problem waiting a bit.

Charlie stirs next to me as I lay my phone down. Brushing her hair away from her face, she greets me with a sleepy smile.

"Morning," she says in a gravelly voice.

"Morning, beautiful. I have to get up and meet with Ozzy."

Her soft lips meet mine and there's nothing I would rather do than recreate all my favorite memories from last night.

"I'll get out of your way," she says, pulling away.

Catching her by the waist, I pull her back to my chest.

"First, I need a shower," I tell her, kissing her again. "Care to join me?"

Her smile is the confirmation I was hoping for. Popping up, I grab Charlie and throw her over my shoulder.

"Linc," she exclaims, smacking my ass.

Naturally, I do the gentlemanly thing and smack hers back.

"Hey!"

"Don't dish it out if you can't take it, babe."

Setting her on the edge of the sink, I turn on the shower to get the water warmed up. While we wait, I stand between her thighs, cupping her face in my palms, and kiss her deeply.

"Mmm," she moans before I lift and carry her into the shower.

"I can walk, you know."

Setting her on her feet, I tilt her head back to the spray.

"True, but then I wouldn't get to have your naked pussy pressed against me."

"You have a filthy mouth." She can pretend to chastise me all she wants, but the gleam in her eye tells me another story.

"You like it," I smile down at her and press my lips to her addictive mouth.

"I do," she concedes.

Pouring my shampoo into her hair, I massage it into her scalp.

"God, that feels so good," she moans as she rinses away the suds. Charlie looks down at my straining cock and her mouth quirks into a half-smile. "There's something we didn't try last night."

"There's a lot we didn't try last night. What is it exactly you're referring to?"

Her hand glides along my shaft and starts pumping up and down.

Standing on her tiptoes, she whispers in my ear, "I had you in my pussy. Now I want you in my mouth."

A deep groan vibrates through my chest when she pulls back and looks up at me, giving me a saucy wink.

"Now, who has the dirty mouth?"

Before she lowers to her knees, I open the shower door, grab a towel, and lay it on the tile.

"Such a gentleman," she quips.

"For you? Absolutely."

We turn in the shower so my back is against the spray, and Charlie sinks to her knees. When her hot mouth wraps around my slick cock, it's everything I can do not to thrust it down her throat.

"Goddamn, baby, that feels so good. Just like that." I pull her wet strands away from her face so I can have a better view as she moves her mouth up and down my length, swirling her tongue around the head every time she reaches the tip. "Open your throat. I want to see how far you can take me." My cock reaches the back of her throat, and instead of gagging like I was worried about, she swallows the head.

"Fuck," I hiss. "You're going to make me come."

Charlie pulls back and gives it another try, taking me even farther. When she lifts her hands and cups my balls, I'm ready to lose it.

"I'm going to come, sweetheart. If you don't want it down your throat, you better move."

Instead, she moans and swallows me again. I shoot off like a fucking rocket, and my girl swallows every last drop.

I lift her from the shower floor and take her mouth in a long and very fucking appreciative kiss that makes her giggle.

"You just blew my fucking mind, and now you're laughing?" I tease, trailing kisses down her neck.

"I'm just surprised you wanted to kiss me... you know, after."

"After you just gave me the best blow job of my fucking life? Yeah, babe, I want to kiss and lick every inch of you, and I don't give a fuck that my cum was just in your mouth." It's a little irritating she would even second-guess that. There's no fucking reason a man shouldn't want to kiss his woman after his dick was in her mouth. Makes me wonder about the asshole who made her think otherwise.

"Actually, I think one good turn deserves another." My lips tilt in a grin. Holding her gaze, I back her up to the shower wall, then lower to my knees and swing her leg over my shoulder.

"That seems fair," she whimpers when I run my tongue through her wet cunt.

I eat her pussy like a starving man, and after she shudders her release against my mouth, I rise to my full height, letting her pull me in for a kiss.

"I like the taste of us just as much as you do, baby," I say, separating my mouth from hers to nuzzle her sweet neck. "There will never be a time when I won't want to kiss you."

Needless to say, it takes a little more than thirty minutes before we leave my room, and I go in search of Ozzy. When Charlie was brushing her teeth and bent over to rinse out her mouth, displaying her sexy-as-fuck naked ass, I had to grab a condom and fuck her one more time against the sink. It was an absolute necessity if you ask me. Ozzy wouldn't understand, so I decide not to mention it to him when I find him in his office.

"Took you long enough."

"Sorry, long night." I move around to the chair in front of his desk and plop down.

"The gossip queens were in a fucking tizzy this morning when Lucy came out for breakfast without Charlie. I'd say I have a pretty good idea of what your night entailed."

The grin that spreads across my face is completely involuntary, and Ozzy rolls his eyes.

"You think this is a wise move on your part?"

"What are you talking about?"

"Linc, the girl just brought a truckload of trouble to the club and still hasn't been forthcoming about what she has. The Italians are on the lookout for her. I doubt they believed me for one second when I told them we don't know her."

"I'll figure it out, Oz. It's not like she's going anywhere."

"Not now that you're sleeping with her, right? You honestly think your dick is that good there's no chance she's gonna get spooked and be in the wind again? She doesn't know the Italians are after her and what they're capable of. The Irish, too, for that matter. The only reason Monaghan isn't up my ass with this is because I told him we have it handled."

"So, if she's here, what's the problem? She'll tell me when she's ready."

"Secrets are no way to start a relationship, Linc. Both of you are keeping shit from each other, and that's dangerous. You can't trust her when she isn't being honest, and it's obvious she doesn't trust you enough to tell you why Jace is really after her."

"I'll talk to her. There's a reason she hasn't said anything. I don't know what she has, but she must be afraid of my reaction if she still hasn't told me." Not that there had been much time for talking last night. "Look, she's just gotten to the point she doesn't look like a scared deer in a clubhouse full of bikers. I just need to build more trust with her. Give it a little time."

"That's something we may not have much of. The Italians aren't known for their patience, and it sounds like whatever she has could do some damage to the Irish. Cataldi reaching out to me tells me they want to take over the guns from the Irish and are ready to take action."

Everything Ozzy's saying makes sense. Charlie needs to come clean. There's more to the story, I'm certain of it. Could she be scared because of our connection to the Irish, and she thinks we'd let something happen to her at their hands? The one thing I know for certain is I need to tread lightly. We may have had an amazing night, but that doesn't mean she trusts me yet.

"Alright, Oz. I'll talk to her."

He nods and dismisses me.

A strong cup of black coffee is needed to attack the rest of this day. When I head toward the kitchen, I hear Stacia's high-pitched, annoying voice.

"Just because you're sleeping with one of the brothers now, don't think you're above cleaning up after them."

"Bitch, you're just mad that paying rent on your back doesn't get you out of cooking and cleaning," I hear Lucy snark.

"Oh, you think your friend is special? Please... last week I was the one—"

I cut off whatever she was about to say when I slam the kitchen door open, startling the three women who look ready to throw down in the middle of the room.

"That's enough, Stacia. Nothing that happens between me and Charlie is any of your fucking business or anyone else's, for that matter. You've been here long enough to know the score. Have a problem with it? Talk to Ozzy. Otherwise, stay the fuck out of Charlie's and Lucy's way."

This drama is the last thing we need first thing in the morning. First, Ozzy getting on my ass about finding out what Charlie has, then I walk into this. I just wanted a cup of coffee and to fuck my girl a few more times before the day is over.

I decide there's only one thing that'll wipe this tension from me.

Tuning to Charlie, I ask, "Ever been on a bike?"

Stacia huffs and stomps out of the kitchen. She's probably pissed I've never offered to take her on a ride.

A wide smile lights up Charlie's face. "No, but I've always wanted to."

"Well, today's your lucky day, Charlie pop."

She laughs, and I tell her to go change into some jeans and boots. I can't help but smack that delicious ass as she walks past me. When I turn to get some coffee before we take off, Lucy is studying me with a warning in her gaze.

"Say it," I tell her.

"Don't mess with my girl's heart, Linc. I know you're doing us a solid by helping us out, but the second I think you're fucking her around, we're out."

"Oh, yeah? And where you gonna go?"

"If you think I can't survive on my own and start over where no one would find us, you're sadly mistaken. I've done it before, and I'll do it again."

Lucy grabs her coffee and leaves the kitchen.

Charlie leaving is exactly what I'm trying to avoid. She needs me. She just has to believe she can trust me.

There's nothing better than the open road with a hot-as-fuck girl's arms wrapped around your middle, hanging on for dear life. I'm not going as fast as usual, but every time I speed up a hair, Charlie squeaks in protest.

We take a long ride around Shine and to the outskirts, where the river runs alongside a little park. I decide this is the perfect place to stop and talk. It's not clear to me how I'm supposed to bring up what Ozzy needs me to. I'm more of a wing-it kind of guy, but Charlie has just now started opening up to me. At least sexually. We still have a pretty far ways to go on all the other stuff. Lucy's words from earlier tumble around in my brain. There's no doubt in my mind she would be able to make good on her threat. What if somehow I make her feel threatened by asking her about what she's hiding? Would she and Lucy take off and put themselves in more danger?

"God, it's so beautiful here. I love being around the water," Charlie says, removing her helmet.

"Yeah this is a great place to find a little peace from the chaos." I grab her helmet and mine, placing them on the handlebars.

"When I first left Liberty, I made it to this little town in Michigan. The lake there was so big, you couldn't see the other side. It's as close to feeling like you're on the ocean as I'll ever get."

"What made you leave?" I ask as we make our way to a little bench on the river's edge.

"The winters," she replies with a laugh.

"It gets pretty cold here too, babe." We sit on the bench, and I throw my arm on the back, playing with the ends of Charlie's dark hair.

"True, but I may be rethinking my stance on cold weather. I'm rethinking my stance on a lot of stuff these days." She sends me a shy smile before turning her gaze back to the river.

"Like what?"

She lets out a sigh before replying.

"It's been just me and Lucy for a long time. I've never had a family like the one you all have made for yourselves. I like it. It's not something I ever let myself consider. When you've never known anything else, you don't expect anything else. Seeing you and your brothers makes me wonder what I've been missing."

"No brothers or sisters, then?"

"No." Charlie laughs. "My mom didn't even want me, really. As soon as I turned eighteen, she was out the door with her trucker boyfriend. She decided she'd done all she needed to by keeping a roof over my head and food in the fridge. It was her turn to live her life and not be tied to the responsibility of a kid."

"Doesn't sound like there was much love in your house." My mom had been a single mom, but we never felt like a burden to her.

"She wasn't a horrible person or anything like that. She didn't hit me or have guys over all the time partying. She just wasn't present, ya know? I was just sort of... there. Like a houseplant. She had to give me water to survive, but other than that, she pretty much ignored me." There's hardly any emotion in Charlie's voice when she talks about her mom, as though she'd become resigned to her mom's indifference long before we crossed paths.

There's a lot my mom probably wished she'd done differently but treating us like we weren't there would never be one of them.

"Then came Jace," she continues, staring out as the river rushes by. "He actually seemed to give a shit about me, at least in the beginning. We were high school sweethearts, and he had a way of making me feel special, seen. Something I wasn't used to." Charlie turns her body toward me.

"You have to understand, it's not like we started dating and he immediately started smacking me around. I'd never really felt loved, like I was important in someone's world. That's exactly what Jace did. His dad was an asshole, so we spent a lot of time at my house. My mom didn't care. I doubt she even noticed. He was the one who took care of me if I got sick or made sure I had cake on my birthday.

"When I turned eighteen, I was still in high school, but that didn't stop my mom from taking off. I had a little money saved up from my after-school job at the diner, and Jace had a job doing oil changes and stuff like that in the only garage our town had. It wasn't much, but we were able to stay in the apartment me and my mom had for a few more months. Jace made sure I wasn't upset by my mom leaving. He told me he loved me every day, and it was like being married. Exactly like I thought it should be. A lot changed after graduation."

When I found Charlie that night all those years ago, she was living in a rundown trailer. Yeah, I'd say a lot changed for her. It's obvious this is the hard part of her story to tell, so I wrap a comforting arm around her, even though anger for her and what she went through courses through me. She doesn't need me going off about what a piece of shit parent her mom was. She obviously came to that conclusion a long time ago. The only thing I can offer now is support while she opens up to me. She gives me one of her sweet smiles, and the urge to kiss her to make her forget the bullshit is strong. I settle for a small peck on the lips because I have to taste her sweetness, then let her continue.

"We moved into the little trailer because rent was so much cheaper. Everything was fine for the first few months. Jace was still working at the garage, and I was able to get more hours at the diner since I wasn't in school. Then he started hanging out with a guy who lived a few spaces down from us. The guy didn't work, but he seemed to have plenty of cash all the time. Said he liked living in the trailer to keep his bills low." Charlie rolls her eyes.

"Jace came home one day and told me he was quitting the garage and was gonna work with this guy. We argued about it because, I don't know, I always got a weird vibe from him. Turns out, he was running meth for a dealer, and Jace decided that was a wise career move for him. He started staying out all night and coming and going at weird hours when he did come home. The changes I saw in him scared me. When I brought it up to him, that was the first time he hit me." A shudder runs through her body.

"Of course, there were apologies and promises to never lay a hand on me again. He was stressed because the guy's supplier was caught and sent to prison. Since they'd already hired someone else at the garage, Jace was broke and jobless. We were living on the tips I made, which wasn't much. Then Jace got in touch with his cousin. He knew Cillian was involved with some less-than-legal activities that brought in major cash in Boston. He would be gone for days at a time, and when he got back, he would crash. God, I remember when I woke him up one time vacuuming." She pauses and takes a deep breath. "Let's just say I'll never look at a vacuum cord the same again."

I don't ask her to elaborate. I don't need to. What I need is to put that fucker six feet under.

"Anyway, it was more of the same. Only difference was he stopped apologizing or making promises."

"I have to tell you, sweetheart, if he wasn't already on my shit list, he sure as hell would be now."

"I felt trapped, ya know? There was no one for me to turn to. He told me plenty of times that he would find me wherever I went. When I came home from work, I'd have to hand over my tips. I was so fucking embarrassed about what my life had become." A tear slips from her eye, which I promptly wipe away with my thumb.

"You have nothing to be embarrassed about, sweetheart. That was all on him."

"I know that now, but it took getting away from him and meeting Lucy before I accepted what he told me was a lie. It wasn't my fault, and no matter what I did to try to make things better and bring the old Jace back, he was gone, replaced by the fucking monster you know now."

"Fuck, Charlie, I'm so thankful I met you that night. If that was what it took for you to get away, I'll never regret spending those six years in prison." The truth of that statement settles down to the marrow of my bones after hearing what she went through.

"When did you meet Lucy?"

She tells me the story of making it to New Orleans, where she stayed for a few years, finally feeling like she was getting her life back and didn't need to be on the run.

"Lucy made me go with her to self-defense classes. She insisted that us girls needed to know how to protect ourselves. I even did some Jiu Jitsu and kickboxing." She lets out a chuckle. "Turns out I'm pretty good."

I raise my eyebrows in surprise. "Really? Well, I think you need to show me what you got then."

Charlie laughs. "I would but I don't want to hurt you."

"Babe, there's nothing you can throw at me that my brother didn't when we were growing up. Trust me, I've been training since I was a kid." I stand and hold my hands out. "Come on, tough girl, let's see what you got."

CHAPTER THIRTEEN
CHARLIE

The idea of grappling with Linc sends excitement shooting through me, especially since he's being a cocky little shit about it.

When I say I took some classes, it meant Lucy and I trained for three years every day. The tourist traps of living in New Orleans lost their shine after about six months. We decided we needed something to spend our days doing since we mostly worked at night. Considering it isn't one of the safest cities in the world and I had no clue how to defend myself physically, Lucy signed me up at her gym. I fell in love with all of it. Taking down people twice my size made me feel ten feet tall. Helping the other women who came to the self-defense class with similar stories to mine and seeing them stand a little taller when they got the hang of it was a high I became addicted to.

Letting Linc pull me up from the bench, I give him a tentative smile.

"You sure?"

A half smirk tilts his lips. "Yeah, babe. I'm sure."

Well, okay then. I'm not going to feel bad about this in the least.

"Come at me like you're going to attack me."

Linc pauses, his cockiness vanishing to be replaced with hesitance.

"It's okay," I reassure him.

He comes at me like he's going to put his hands around my throat. When Linc makes contact, I use my arms to cover my face and rotate quickly on my back leg, breaking his hold, then holding his arms with one of mine before driving my other elbow into his nose.

Of course, I don't actually hit him, I don't want to hurt the poor guy. It all happens so fast, he's stunned still for a moment before a wide smile stretches across his face.

"Impressive."

"Now grab me from behind, but put a little more effort into it," I tell him with a wink.

He laughs and shakes his head. "Okay."

Linc comes up behind me and grabs me from behind, circling his arms fully around me. I bend over and set my base, pushing my hips back into him, and grab his leg. Losing his balance, he falls back, and I hold his leg in a knee lock.

"Holy shit, babe. Nice job," he says when I turn to him with a huge smile.

I release his leg, and he hops back up.

"Okay, now grab me in a headlock from behind."

Linc does just that, and I grab his arm, pulling it down and tucking my chin. Throwing my hips back as I bend my knees and throw my upper body into a fold, I use the momentum to throw him over my shoulder. This one is great because it works when your attacker is bigger by using both of your momentum to execute the move. Plus, I like shocking the shit out of people when they go flying through the air.

Linc lands on his back and the air whooshes from him.

"Okay," he coughs out. "I believe you."

I hold out my hand to help him up, but he pulls me down on top of him then rolls me under him.

"Can you get out of this one?" he asks, smiling down at me.

"I could," I tell him, throwing my arms around his shoulders. "But I don't want to."

Linc leans down and kisses me solidly on the mouth as I wrap my legs around his waist.

"Gotta say, babe, being beat to shit by you is more of a turn-on than I would have imagined."

"You don't have to say it. I can feel it." I roll my hips into his erection.

He lets out a low groan and grinds into me, kissing me senseless.

Suddenly, a car horn sounds, and both of us look over at a woman pulling up in a minivan with a disapproving scowl on her face.

"Busted," he laughs out, popping to his feet and holding out a hand to help me up.

I swipe at the grass all over my back side, and Linc comes around to inspect.

"Missed a spot," he says, grabbing a handful of my ass.

Looking over to the minivan now parked in the lot, I see a bunch of kids piling out and the woman standing next to the door with her arms crossed over her chest, giving us the stink eye.

"We should probably get out of here before she calls the police on us for indecent exposure or something."

Linc looks over at her and laughs. "You're probably right. There's definitely nothing decent about what I want to do to you right now." He grabs me again and kisses me deeply. "One more for the road."

We make our way back to the bike sweaty and happy.

"Feel like grabbing some food?" he asks as we settle onto the bike.

"Sure," I reply. "Especially if dessert is involved."

"Dessert is always involved." He turns his head and wiggles his eyebrows in a suggestive manner.

"Perv." I smack his chest.

"And proud."

The roar of the engine drowns out the retort on my tongue as we head back into town. Linc pulls up to a tiny local diner that looks like it dates back to the sixties, complete with checkered floors, red vinyl booths, and those little jukeboxes on each table.

"Hey, Linc. Anywhere you want," the waitress calls from behind the counter.

We settle into a booth near the back of the diner before the only waitress in the place brings us a couple menus and a cup of coffee for Linc.

"What'll you have to drink?" she asks me.

"Coffee, too, please."

She turns to Linc. "You having your usual?"

He nods. "Two, please."

When the waitress walks away, I shoot him a glare.

"Um, excuse you. I'm perfectly capable of ordering for myself. What if I don't like whatever your usual is?"

"Trust me, Charlie bear."

"I thought I vetoed that one?"

"Thought I'd give it another shot." Linc shrugs a shoulder and winks.

The man is impossible.

"So, you came to Shine from Nebraska?"

"Yup. Mom moved out there from Knoxville before I was born."

"Ah, that explains Knox then. And Linc. Short for Lincoln?"

"Yup. Real original, my mom," he remarks and lets out a chuckle.

"Aw, I think it's cute."

He laughs. "It's never bothered me. What's in a name? Knox used to get irritated because people would call him Tennessee. Then again, there wasn't much that didn't irritate Knox when we were growing up."

That doesn't surprise me when I think about the aloof biker who only seemed to soften when I saw him with his mom.

"What made your mom move from Tennessee to Nebraska? That's a big change."

"She met my dad. He got a job out there, and they decided a fresh start would be good for them. She had Knox right out of high school and was a single mom until my dad came around. He wasn't the nicest man."

That's the sense I got when Tanya and I talked for a few moments the other night. I had no idea he was Linc's dad, though.

"He beat the shit out of my mom, but would usually leave us alone. She kicked him out so many damn times, but he would come around asking for money and refusing to leave until she gave him some. One night, she put her foot down, and he decided to take it out on my brother. I jumped on his back, and he threw me off. I landed headfirst into the coffee table." Linc pulls his hair back and shows me the faint scar on his hair line. "Mom hit him in the head with a pan, and he ran out the door. That night she packed us up, and we started driving."

"Wow, I had no idea." I take a sip of my coffee. "Did you ever hear from your dad again?"

"He came to find us a couple years later. I guess he got in contact with my mom's sister. Her sister thought he'd changed or something. Turns out he didn't." Linc clenches his jaw like he's chewing on his next words. "He followed my mom home from work one day and broke into our house. From what I gather, he was trying to make her pack and convince her to go back to Nebraska. She could tell he was unhinged and high on something. At first, she played along 'til she could get away and call for help. He ran out to his car to grab something, and she took her chance to run out the back door. She didn't make it past the backyard before he caught her and dragged her back in the house."

The fear his mom must have felt is so similar to what I've felt myself many times over. That moment right before a beating when you know it's going to happen, and you can't escape it.

"He started wailing on her, just beating the hell out of her. Knox and I walked in and saw him on top of her punching her head while she tried to fight him off and protect herself at the same time." His eyes close, reliving the memory of a young boy seeing his mother being beaten by his father. A man who was supposed to protect them. It's absolutely heart-wrenching to witness.

"We liked to play baseball at the little league field down the street, so there was a bat by the door. God, my mom would always yell at us to put our stuff away, that she was tired of tripping over it all the time." He lets out a huff. "I'm glad as hell we didn't listen. Knox picked up the bat and swung it across that fucker's head. Knocked him off our mom and knocked him out cold. I called Trick, then we grabbed our mom and ran out front to wait for him." A small spread across Linc's lips.

"It didn't take more than two minutes for Trick and three other brothers to show up. My dad was still knocked out cold in our living room. They hauled him into a van and sped off. Trick stayed with my mom and cleaned her cuts while she sobbed. Fuck, that was hard to see." He pauses, taking a long sip of his coffee.

"Gramps and Janine showed up a little while later. My brother and I were sitting on the stairs in front of the house when Trick came out. That was the first time I saw him as more than my friend's dad. When he walked out, he was every inch the MC president. He looked at us and said, 'Good job calling me. You always call family when you're in trouble. That man is not your family, and you'll never see him again.'" Linc sits back in the booth and shrugs his shoulders.

"And we never did. That night, Gramps decided to teach us how to fight 'London style,' he called it." He barks out a laugh. "It wasn't much different from how we messed around, only a whole hell of a lot dirtier." When a smile lights up his face, I see the respect and love he has for the man he calls Gramps.

"So, that's my sad story. That's why I love the club and everyone in it like family. From that day forward, I had a real family who would put themselves in the line of fire for me, and I'd do the same for them."

"And that's why when you saw me, you couldn't turn a blind eye."

Linc nods. "That's exactly why. It's also why I'll protect my brothers until my dying breath."

The waitress comes back with two bacon cheeseburgers the size of my head and a huge portion of fries for each of us. My eyes are the size of saucers when I see the gigantic meal.

"You like to eat, and I like to feed you. Told you that you'd like it." A wide grin overtakes Linc's face as he picks up the burger. "Best burgers in Shine."

I take a bite of mine and groan in agreement. "You're not wrong."

Conversation is nonexistent as we devour the food in front of us. When we're finished, Linc asks me if I'm ready for dessert.

"How can you possibly consider more food after that?" I wave my hand at his plate.

The devious twinkle in his eye tells me he wasn't referring to food.

"You're insatiable," I say with a giggle.

"Only for you, babe." The sexy wink he gives me causes butterflies to riot low in my belly.

Linc throws a few twenties on the table, enough to cover our tab and leave a generous tip. Getting back on his bike, I lean forward and brush my lips against his neck.

"Thank you for today and for telling me about everything," I whisper before he starts the bike.

"Days not over yet." He starts his bike and calls back, "Hold on tight."

Linc peels out of the parking lot, and I let out a cross between a laugh and a yelp. We're going faster than earlier, but instead of being scared out of my mind, I relax into him and let the freedom of being with him wash over me.

As Linc speeds through the mostly empty street, I notice a black sedan keeping pace with us. I tap Linc's shoulder and point my thumb over my shoulder. Just as he looks in his side mirror, the car turns down a neighborhood street and out of our sight.

When we arrive back at the clubhouse, Linc asks me about the car.

"I mean, it might not have been following us, just looked a little out of place." I shake out my hair and try to finger-comb the knots. Note to self: next time, put my hair in a braid, not a ponytail. "Sorry if it seemed like I was freaking out over nothing."

"No, babe," he starts leading me to the door. "Those are good instincts. Always tell me if something seems a little off, no matter how small you think it is."

I smile at him as he opens the door.

"This is absolute bollocks," comes an angry British voice when I step into the clubhouse. "A bunch of shite, I tell you," Jude swears as I watch him unbuckle his belt and whip it out of the loops before setting it in the middle of the table in front of him.

A loud laugh escapes me when I take in the scene before me. There are four bikers, all in various stages of undress, sitting at a card table with my best friend, still fully clothed.

Ozzy and Knox are sitting at the bar with smirks on their faces when they see Linc and me enter the room.

"What the hell... Never mind, I don't think I want to know," Linc says from behind me.

"The boys decided they wanted to play a game of poker. Not sure which one thought strip poker was a good idea," Knox tells him.

"In our defense, we didn't realize Lucifer was a bloody card shark," Jude grouses.

"Don't blame me just because you thought I was bad at poker," Lucy says. "What was it you said?" she asks while tapping her chin with her cards. "Oh, yeah, there's no way a bloody bird can play better than us. It'll be like stealing candy from a baby," she says, badly mimicking Jude's accent.

"One." Jude holds up a finger. "I don't sound like that. And two,"—he holds up another finger—"you made it seem like you'd never played a day in your life."

"I never said that," Lucy replies. "I just told you I don't really like playing. It's not my strong suit. You decided that meant I didn't know what I was doing and decided strip poker would be a fun way to pass the time. Sorry, pal, you never asked if I was good. I just don't really like card games. Doesn't mean I don't know how to play them." The small smile on her face tells me she isn't sorry in the least.

"Well, I think I'm done embarrassing myself," Barrett says. He's the one who looks as though he lost the most hands, with only a bandanna covering his lap. "I know when to call it."

He stands, keeping the small piece of fabric in place as he rifles through the pile on the table, grabbing his pants, shirt, and black boxer briefs. When he turns to leave, he gives the entire room a full view of his ass as he walks back toward the bedrooms. Linc promptly covers my eyes with his large hand, his deep laugh vibrating through his chest.

"Your friend is a menace," he whispers in my ear.

"She absolutely is." A light giggle slips out of me when he nips at my ear.

"I think I promised you dessert earlier." His thumb brushes the skin under my shirt right above the button of my jeans.

The tantalizing movement causes a rush of tingles just south of where his finger is caressing.

"Give me a minute. I'm gonna check in with Lucy."

Linc kisses the side of my neck and releases his hold on me. "Meet me in my room."

I nod and make my way to Lucy.

"You good?" I take a look at her hand and Jude's glowering expression. He's about to lose what little he has on.

"Oh, yeah. Don't worry about me, sis. Go have fun." She looks up at me and shoots me a salacious wink. When her gaze travels across the table to Jude, she announces, "You know what, maybe I do like playing cards after all."

Jude mumbles something about liking the pits of hell, and I laugh, heading in the direction of Linc's room. Maybe one of these days, those two will get along.

Not today, though.

CHAPTER FOURTEEN
CHARLIE

I head back to my room before going to Linc's. Seeing as this was my first time on a bike, I wanted to make sure I didn't have any bugs in my teeth or something equally embarrassing.

When I look at myself in the mirror, the carefree smile reflecting back is almost unrecognizable. I've never seen a smile on my face this bright before. The shooting lessons, the grappling in the park, the kisses, all of it is making me feel like a complete badass.

Laughing at myself as I brush my teeth, I think about last night. Sweet Jesus, my body has never come alive like that. I'd accepted a long time ago that sex wasn't the end all be all so many romance books made it out to be. Granted, I'd only gone all the way with one man. I'd had a brief flirty encounter with a guy in New Orleans. It ended with a sloppy makeout session where he tried to take it further. The fumbling around in the dark and his trying to find my clit with his fingers were thankfully interrupted when Lucy came home early from a shift. It was awkward and mildly embarrassing, but there was no desire on my end to try again with him or anyone else, for that matter.

Not Linc, though. He had no problem finding every part of me that made me light up and beg for more.

When I knock on his bedroom door, Linc calls for me to come in.

I open the door and find him lounging on his bed with his bare feet crossed at the ankles.

"Hey, babe." He sends me a panty-melting grin and crooks his finger, beckoning me to him. There's something so casually sexy, if that's even a thing, about seeing him relaxed in his space. It makes me want to crawl up his body and tuck myself as far into him as I can get.

When I'm close enough, he jackknifes up and grabs my hand, pulling me over him. I let out a yelp and laugh.

"I love that sound."

"What? The sound of you scaring the shit out of me?" I tease.

"No," he says, brushing my dark locks out of my face. "The sound of you happy." His hand cups the side of my face, and he pulls me in for a toe-curling kiss. Oh, who am I kidding? Every kiss from him curls my toes.

With my legs on either side of his, he grabs my ass and rubs my center over the bulge in his jeans.

"Feel what you do to me," he whispers as he traces warm, wet kisses down the column of my throat. "I want to touch you everywhere. Kiss every inch of your tempting fucking body."

His words make me feel brazen and needy.

"Mmm, baby. Just like that," he groans out as I rub myself faster on him, spurred on by the desperation in his voice.

"Sit up."

I do as he says, and he whips my shirt over my head, throwing it somewhere in his room. Linc pulls down the lace covering my oversensitive nipples, too impatient to take my bra off before attaching his mouth and sucking. My hands tangle in his soft hair, and I cry out in pleasure.

"I love it when you make those noises, Charlie. You like my mouth on these pretty little nipples?"

"God, yes," I say on a breathy moan.

His mouth moves to the other, and he gives it a little bite. I let out a squeal of surprise as he laves the abused nipple with his tongue.

"Fuck, baby, if you keep rubbing on me, I'm going to come in my pants like a goddamn teenager." He finally undoes the clasp of my bra, letting it fly somewhere in the direction of my shirt. "These need to come off," he says, undoing the button of my jeans.

I lift up as he wrenches the pants down my hips and thighs. Linc pulls me back to his chest, and we're a tangle of wet kisses and rough hands trying to get my pants all the way off. When the offending denim finally gets low enough, I kick them off my feet, and I'm completely naked on top of Linc, who's still fully clothed.

"Come up here, baby. I want you to sit on my face."

There's something downright dirty about being stripped down to nothing with him still having all his clothes on. Like I'm his naked toy, and he wants to play.

Crawling up his chest and over his shoulders, I settle my knees on either side of his head, feeling slightly self-conscious about having my pussy directly over his face. This is all new to me, and I'm not quite sure what I'm supposed to do.

"Hold on to the headboard and get closer."

I do as he says and lower myself a couple inches.

"Baby, when I said sit on my face, it means I want you to smother me with that perfect pussy." He grabs my hips and sits me fully on his face, moaning into me. His tongue spears my center, and I cry out.

He eats at me with a ferocity I've never felt before, as if he is making a full meal out of me. His tongue is everywhere, tasting every part of me. His groans of satisfaction spur me on, and I begin rubbing my pussy on him. Holy fuck, this feels so good. My fingernails dig into the headboard, surely leaving marks as I clutch it tightly. Linc's hand kneads my ass as a finger finds the sensitive pucker of my ass and presses.

When he latches onto my clit, he sucks as his tongue moves furiously over the overly sensitive bud. All the sensations coming at me from everywhere all at once are almost too much. It only takes moments before I detonate, the orgasm ripping through my body and nearly causing me to fall over.

Linc takes a last lick through my center, groaning again. Lifting me from his face, he pulls me down his body, our lips nearly touching. His mouth is glistening with the evidence of my orgasm. His fingers tangle in the back of my hair as he closes the small gap between us, thrusting his tongue into my mouth.

"I want your taste on my tongue every fucking day, Charlie. You've turned me into a goddamn addict for your pussy." He flips us over and sits up, ripping his shirt off as he goes.

"I need to be inside you." There's a desperation in his voice and movements I've never experienced before. Everything about him is screaming with urgency to take, to fill, to completely turn my world on its axis.

I'm still a trembling mess of need as he stands and lowers his jeans, his cock on display right in front of my face. Lifting my head, I swirl the crown with my tongue before slipping it in my mouth and taking him as far down my throat as I can.

Linc's hands grab the side of my face as he pumps in and out of my mouth.

"Goddamn, baby, your mouth feels too good."

His words of praise flow through me, shining light into every dark part of me that had me convinced for years I wasn't good enough or sexy enough. That I was simply an object to be used, then discarded when I served my purpose. Linc needs my pleasure, begs for it even. He revels in the different ways he finds to make my body sing with his touch, his tongue, his cock.

Pulling away, he grabs a condom from the bedside table and sheathes himself before crawling between my thighs.

"Look at you," he says, running a hand from my neck to my pussy, using one finger to circle my clit. "So ready for me to fill this pussy with my cock."

"Linc, please," I beg, needing to feel him connected to me.

"I've got you, Charlie."

He positions himself at my entrance and slowly pushes inside of me, groaning as he moves along my walls until he's fully in. I squeeze my eyes shut, so overcome with the sensation of being filled by him. Linc lowers himself over me, slowly pulling out and pushing back inside. His movements aren't quick, not as I anticipated moments ago, but they are deep. So fucking deep.

"Open your eyes, baby." When I do, he smiles down at me, our noses almost touching. "There you are. Do you feel how deep I am? How good your pussy swallows my cock?"

"God, yes. It feels so good," I whimper.

He quickens his pace, still thrusting deep.

"I need you to come, baby." His finger swirls around my clit over and over. "I need to feel you strangle my cock when I come inside you." Linc presses his forehead to mine, locking his eyes with my own. "That's it. You're almost there, aren't you?"

I nod as my walls begin to flutter.

"Yes, right there. Oh, fuck," I yell into his room as he thrusts into me, taking me to the peak. I fall over the edge again as Linc crashes his mouth to mine, our moans mixing with our kiss.

When he pulls out, he discards the condom, then lies on his back, pulling me across his sweaty chest. His fingertips softly brush through my hair as we both catch our breath.

"I hope you know I'm never letting you go," he says.

Before, in another life with another person, that statement would have sent fear skittering through me. But here and now, in this room, there's no place for fear. Only blissful happiness.

There's only me and Linc.

I spent the night in Linc's room again. It was early when we came back from our ride, so after a nap, Linc got up and grabbed us some sandwiches. Before he got back, I texted Lucy to make sure she was okay without me.

Me: *Hey, you good out there? Need me to come rescue you?*

Lucy: *Psh. Please, girl. These boys are the ones who'll need rescuing when I annihilate their asses in quarters. The Brit is determined to find a game I can't beat him at.*

I laugh and shake my head. He's going to be trying for a very long time.

Me: *Ok. Let me know if you need me.*

Lucy: *The only thing I need is for you to let me concentrate and have fun with your own biker. I'm busy showing this one who's boss.*

She ends her text with a smiley face.

The next morning, Linc is called to church. Before we part ways, he leaves me with a scorching kiss that holds wicked promises of things to come.

I find Lucy in the kitchen pouring coffee for a couple of the guys who look a lot worse for wear.

"I take it you won." I smile, coming to stand next to her.

"Of course, I did." She winks and hands Barret and Wyatt a cup of strong black coffee. "They'll learn, eventually."

Both men let out a grunt of appreciation and head to the meeting with the other brothers. We take our cups out into the main room, settling into one of the large leather couches.

"So," she says, nudging my arm. "You spent another night in your biker's bed. He must really be something else." Her eyebrows wiggle up and down as she smiles at me.

There is absolutely no way to keep the grin off my face as I sip the magic bean juice, otherwise known as coffee.

"Ladies don't kiss and tell."

"True, but we do."

I laugh at her insistence. I've never been with any-one since knowing Lucy, so confiding in my best friend about my love life is completely new territory for me.

"Pretty soon, you'll be throwing bunnies out on their asses like Tanya when one tried to get too close to Trick."

It hits me then. A memory from the notebook. O and T. Ozzy and Trick. That's what it has to be. It would be too much of a coincidence for it *not* to be them.

Trick was the president of the club when Linc went to prison, and Ozzy was the vice president. They already said they had dealings with the Irish. That means not only was Jace keeping tabs on the mafia but also on a criminal motorcycle club. I have evidence in my pos-session that any number of their enemies or the D.A. would love to get their hands on.

I need to give him the notebook. It's bad enough I've kept it from him this long, especially after yesterday when he opened up to me about so much. It's not like he's going to hand me over to the Irish with the note-book now, right? I know this thing between us is new, but I know I can at least trust that.

"Lucy, I think I figured something out."

"That I'm a total genius, and you should always take my advice, especially when it comes to men?"

"About the notebook," I whisper.

That wipes the smile off her face, and she listens intently to my suspicions.

"I have to tell him, right?"

Lucy sways her head back and forth, considering my question.

"Do you trust him enough to tell him the truth? That you know a lot more about the Irish and his club than what you've been letting on."

I think about that for a moment. "Yes, I do. He'll know I didn't have any clue how involved they were, and I think it would be worse if I didn't tell him. It's not like Jace is going to give up. The longer I hold on to it, the more trouble the club could be in because of me."

"Then I think you have your answer. These guys seem pretty reasonable, aside from Jude," she grumbles. "As long as you're straight with them about what you figured out, it's not a stretch to think they'll handle the Jace situation."

I think about last night when Linc told me he was keeping me. He wouldn't say it if he didn't mean it. I have to trust him to know I would've never done anything with that damn notebook to hurt him or his brothers.

"Well, isn't this cute?" Stacia calls as she walks to the couch Lucy and I are sitting on. "I hope you're ready to get kicked out on your asses. Word around is you brought trouble with you, Charlie. Ozzy isn't going to be too eager to clean up your mess now that the Italians are involved."

"What the hell are you talking about?" Lucy sneers.

"They're in a meeting right now, trying to figure out what to do with you. I don't know the specifics, but if I was you, I'd pack my shit and hit the road. There's been enough problems with the Italians in the past, and Trick and Ozzy have worked hard to keep the peace. No way is he going to let you come in and ruin it."

Lucy stands from her seat. "Shut your dumb mouth, bitch. You have no idea what you're talking about. Linc wants her here, and Ozzy okayed that decision. Seems you're the only one who's got a problem with it, and I highly doubt he takes advice from you."

"Fuck you, bitch. You think you and your friend are so superior to any of us just because she's sleeping with one of them," she yells, pointing at me. "You'll both be gone like yesterday's trash soon enough. Just wait 'til they get out of church."

"Stacia, don't talk about things you don't have the first clue about," the prospect calls from the bar. "I'll tell you one thing, Ozzy hates bunny drama more than anything else, so I'd watch your mouth if I were you."

"Shut up, prospect. You don't know shit."

"That's enough," Ozzy hollers from the doorway leading from where they hold church. "Stacia, I've had about enough of your shit. You should already know better than to disrespect any member, prospect, or guest of this club. Since you can't seem to remember your place, I'll make it real clear for you. You don't have one. Get your shit and get the hell out of my club."

Stacia looks at Ozzy, shock written across her face. Guess she didn't think they would be done so soon.

"Ozzy—" she starts.

"I'm certain I didn't ask you to argue." He points down the hallway with narrowed eyes and a tight jaw, and she scrambles to her room.

Linc is behind Ozzy, watching as his former fuck buddy, or maybe it would be considered fuck bunny, is getting thrown out on her ass. Not a shred of sympathy shows on his face. In fact, no emotion whatsoever is in his gaze. It's weird and so at odds with the eyes I'm used to looking into. The man doesn't necessarily wear his heart on his sleeve, but this is something different, something colder.

When he turns to face me, though, his expression changes. Instead of cold indifference, there's heated anger, and it's directed at me.

CHAPTER FIFTEEN
UNC

Leaving my bed this morning was a true testament of my will and commitment to my club. Damn, Charlie's naked form lying peacefully next to me was enough to make me almost tell Ozzy to fuck off when he called church at stupid early a.m. The only thing I wanted was to have some sleepy good morning sex with my girl, not sit in a room of grumpy bikers, who are as much morning people as I am.

But duty fucking calls, so my ass is in the seat next to Knox, waiting for the rest of my brothers to hobble in.

"You look like shit," I say to Wyatt and Barrett as they trudge to the table. When Jude enters church after them, it's all I can do not to laugh. He sinks to his seat with sunglasses over his eyes and an almost green pallor to his skin. "Rough night?" I laugh, not being able to control it.

"Your girl's friend is the Devil incarnate, and nothing you say will make me believe otherwise."

I chuckle again at his obvious discomfort from not being able to sleep off what looks to be the hangover from hell.

"I thought you Brits were immune to hangovers or some shit."

"Obviously, you thought wrong." Jude shakes his head. "I've never seen a woman so good at quarters. It's like she willed the damn coin to make it in the cup every time. It's unnatural. She's gotta be some sort of telekinetic demon."

When the rest of the brothers wander in, Ozzy bangs the gavel on the table harder than usual, which elicits a groan from the three hungover fools who had something to prove with Lucy last night.

Idiots.

"Got word from the Irish late last night. Seems Cillian heard from his cousin." Ozzy gives me a look that isn't hard to interpret. He's irritated they have information about this situation that we still don't, and it's my fault.

"I was planning on talking to Charlie about it today, Oz."

After last night, it finally feels like she's ready to trust me, not just with her body but her secrets as well.

"Be that as it may, Jace has enlisted the Italians. He called Cillian and warned him that a war was coming, and he was going to be on the losing side. The guy was high as a fucking kite, according to him. Told Cillian that Charlie has a notebook containing dates, names, and places of some deals. Also, the routes the Irish used to push product to Canada and the location of several safe houses."

"How the hell did that fucking guy get so much info?" Knox asks.

"Cillian had him doing odd jobs of the illegal variety for a while when the Irish didn't want to be directly involved," Ozzy answers. "Unfortunately for everyone, seems this fucker was keeping track of the people he met and the places he went. He told Cillian that he had a bunch of shit on us, too. Said the Italians were more than happy to cut a deal with him in exchange for the information in the notebook Charlie stole from him."

"Why did he give his cousin a heads-up? He knows we're on good terms with the Irish," Jude chimes in, finally joining the land of the living.

"Cillian says he's gone off the rails. That's why he stopped throwing work his way years ago. He saw the writing on the wall and didn't want Jace involved with his business anymore."

"By writing on the wall, does he mean he knew his cousin was beating the shit out of Charlie?" The idea enrages me. I always liked Cillian, so I'd hate to have to come to blows with him. And I would if he knew what that fuckhead was doing to her and didn't step in.

"I don't think so. We all know Cillian. He's a good man who runs a tight crew. If he knew one of his employees was beating on a woman, he'd make damn sure to put a stop to it, family or not."

I nod in agreement. From what I remember, Charlie only met the guy once or twice. She could have very well been hiding her bruises like she tried to do at the diner the first time I met her.

"Where is this little fucker then?" Barrett asks.

"Cillian isn't sure. He could be holed up in some Italian safe house for all we know. If they think he has the information to bring down the Irish and us, they'll probably be keeping close tabs on him." Ozzy looks at me. "My question is, why hasn't she handed the notebook over to us."

"I don't know," I answer honestly. Why hasn't she seen fit to trust me? I've never given her reason to doubt me; the opposite, in fact. Now that Jace is calling in threats and making deals with our enemies, it's vital now more than ever she stops thinking me or my brothers wouldn't protect her.

"I guess my question is, why did she grab it in the first place? Was she biding her time until she was in a position to turn it over to the authorities? Maybe that's why she was so quick to hop in the van, then on your dick? Maybe she's been trying to gather more information or trying to get you to trust her to see what other tidbits she could gather," Jude says.

"I'm going to assume you're still drunk, asshole, and that's why you're spouting off this nonsense," I shoot back at him.

"Sorry, brother,"—he holds up his hands—"but we need to look at all the angles. She has shit that could get this entire club thrown in prison for the rest of our lives and hasn't exactly been forthcoming about it. Hell, if Cillian hadn't reached out to us, we would have no idea what was really going on between her and her ex."

I'm about to lose my shit on my best friend. Partly because this is the same bullshit he was saying when we were in Texas and partly because I'm afraid he's right. It doesn't make sense why Charlie hasn't said anything to me about the notebook, and I've been too wrapped up in her to take a closer look at that.

"Linc, you need to get whatever she has today. I don't care if she denies having anything. If she does, we'll toss her room and find it ourselves. I'm tired of being a sitting duck." Ozzy slams the gavel and dismisses church.

As soon as he opens the door, we hear yelling from the main room.

Sounds like Stacia is talking about shit she should have no knowledge of, considering her place in this clubhouse.

I see Lucy standing in front of the soon-to-be for-mer bunny, squaring off with her in defense of her best friend, who is watching the exchange like a damn ping-pong match. When Stacia tells the prospect be-hind the bar to fuck off, Ozzy loses it and tells her she's outstayed her usefulness.

Good riddance.

My eyes find Charlie, and Jude's questions run through my mind. I don't think she had plans to turn the notebook over to anyone, but why does she still have it? Why not come clean with me about it a couple days ago? How well do I really know her? Enough to trust her with the lives of my brothers?

When I make my way over to her, she stands, concern etched on her face.

"Linc, what's wrong?"

"We need to talk."

"Does this have to do with what Stacia was going on about?"

A humorless laugh escapes me. "You know, it's funny you should ask that. Maybe Ozzy is kicking out the wrong girl." I don't know where this anger is suddenly coming from. Maybe the doubts I have stem from the fear that Jude's suspicions were on the money all along. I hate being afraid of anything, almost more than I hate the idea of Jude being right.

"Listen, I need to tell you something," she says, urgency lacing her tone.

"Does it have to do with a notebook you've been hiding from all of us about the dealings the club has had with the Irish?" Her wide-eyed expression of surprise would be funny when I mention the notebook if I wasn't so pissed right now.

"Yes, but I didn't know—"

"Know what? That you have information that could land my brothers in prison? Me back in prison?" I ask harshly, cutting her off before she can justify her lies.

"I didn't know about the connection to the club."

I give her a dubious look.

"Linc, you have to believe me," she implores. "It *just* registered what a lot of stuff in that book meant. He used initials for a lot of names, including anything having to do with your club."

"Why didn't you tell me that's what he was after, Charlie? Why keep this huge thing from me?"

"What should I have done, Linc?" She holds out her hands, exasperation radiating from her body. "I didn't know you were mentioned in that book, but I knew the Irish were. The first time I saw you after six years and that asshole found me, you acted like you were scared of who his cousin was. If Cillian would've known what I had, who would be there to stop him from hunting me down and killing me?"

"I would! Do you really think I would have let anyone hurt you? I went to prison for six years because that piece of shit was putting his hands on you. Do you actually believe I would have gone through all of that just to hand you back over to someone who's hurt you or worse?" Linc shakes his head. "Jesus fuck, woman, who do you think I am?"

"Linc, I didn't know what to think. Honestly, at first I was scared you were there for the notebook."

"If you didn't know we were mentioned in it, why would you think that?"

"I don't know!" she exclaims, throwing her arms in the air. "There were a million things going on in my mind. We had only been in Texas for a few months, and we left New Orleans because I saw Jace's cousin across the street from my work. I thought he'd come after me because I knew too much or something."

I let out a caustic laugh. "Fuck Charlie, this isn't the fucking movies. He would have given you the opportunity to come clean. We may be criminals, but we aren't fucking monsters."

"How in the hell was I supposed to know that? The only criminal I'd ever known *was* a fucking monster, Linc. It's not a stretch to think I needed to protect myself after what I'd been through."

I shake my head, disappointment rolling through my chest and filling up that part of me I let her into.

"I have never shown you anything but kindness, Charlie. I wanted you to believe there were good men out there, that I was a good man, and you could trust me."

"I do, Linc. That's why I was going to tell you about everything today. As soon as you were done with church, I was going to tell you what I had."

"I don't know if I believe you Charlie. I still don't understand why you didn't tell me in the first place. You, more than anyone else on this planet, know what I would do to protect you. What I would give up to make sure you were safe. Why you couldn't give me just a little bit of trust to do it again is what's killing me right now."

She reaches her hand to mine, but I quickly rip it from her grasp as though I've been burned.

"I need to go and clear my head," I tell her as Lucy comes to Charlie's side. "You aren't to leave the clubhouse until I get back."

Lucy opens her mouth to argue, I'm sure to tell me she can do whatever she damn well pleases, but Charlie shakes her head at her friend.

"I'll be here when you get back."

I nod and head to my bike. I need a long ride to clear the shit rolling around in my brain.

The winding roads of Massachusetts are doing their job. I'm calmer than when I left the clubhouse, but the questions still circulate. More than that even, it's disappointment. Disappointment in Charlie for not trusting me and disappointment in myself for going off on her the way I did. I've always considered myself a pretty level-headed guy. Sure, I have my triggers, anyone hurting women being the main one, but other than that, I like to think I'm reasonable, yet Charlie was afraid to tell me about that damn notebook.

Taking into account her past and no one giving a shit about her, how could I really expect her to? All she knew about me that night in Texas was I was in a MC. Sure, she knew I'd gone to prison to protect her, but seeing me beat the shit out of her ex probably hadn't instilled much confidence in me or the club, if I'm being honest with myself. It really wasn't until yesterday that she understood the depth of our loyalty to each other and those we consider family.

Does Charlie even know that's what the club sees her as now? Probably not. It sure as shit snuck up on me. I never wanted to be tied down to one woman, especially after prison. It didn't seem worth it to have an old lady when I knew any day the police could come knocking and haul me away in handcuffs. I saw what the visits did to my mom and couldn't fathom being in that situation with a woman of my own.

But then I saw Charlie again. I'll never forget the way her bright blue eyes were round as saucers when she recognized me. All I could think was, damn, the years have done her good. Gone was the skinny little thing I saw beat down in a diner. This new Charlie had a fierceness about her that called to me.

When she heard about Jace tracking her down, she was ready and able to take off again. There was no way she was going to be taken back into that kind of situation. She had to reinvent herself so many times before I found her, but she refused to be his victim again. She was doing the best she knew how to, and it was working for her.

I don't regret finding her in Texas. Fuck, if we hadn't, who knows what would have happened to her. I don't regret bringing her back to Shine with us, even though it's bringing some heat from the Italians. The only thing I regret is Charlie still doesn't trust me to have her back. The club I can understand because she doesn't know most of the guys. But me? Yeah, that one stings.

My bike is heading in the direction of my mom's place she shares with Trick and Gramps. If anyone can help me make sense of what Charlie has been feeling, it's the woman who was in the same situation when I was a kid. She must hear my bike rumbling up the long drive because she's on the porch waiting for me.

"Well, this is a surprise," my mom calls when I park and turn off the engine.

I take a few long strides and pick her up in a huge hug.

"Put me down, ya big oaf," she laughs out.

When I set her on her feet, her scrutinizing gaze collides with mine. She gives me that look only the person who raised you and knows you better than anyone else can.

"What's going on?"

"Stuff with Charlie. I think I messed up."

"Already?" she asks with a teasing smile. "Okay, come in and get some coffee. I don't expect Trick and Gramps back for a few hours yet."

We walk into the two-story farmhouse where Ozzy grew up. Shit, my brother and I were regular fixtures here too. Janine and Gramps had built the house when Trick was a baby. After Knox and I graduated high school, Mom and Trick decided to come clean about their relationship. I still find it ridiculous they waited so long, but my mom wanted to make sure we knew we were her priority.

"Sit. I'll make us some coffee." She brings the steaming mugs over and has a seat across from me. "So, what's going on?" Her "mom fixer face" is in place as she takes a drink of her coffee.

"Some shit followed Charlie from Texas. She was holding some information close to her chest, and it's put the club in a tough spot." I sip from my mug before setting it on the table in front of me and running a hand over my face. "If she would have confided in me in the first place, we could have handled it. Instead, Ozzy and some of the other brothers feel blindsided."

"Did you expect her to trust you right away?"

"I mean, rationally, I know you have to build up to that, but I've never given her a reason not to."

"Sweetie, see if from her perspective." My mom gives me a patient smile. "She was on the run from a man and a life that almost killed her. Then you run into her out of the blue, and the only thing she knows about you is you went to prison for saving her and that she ran before she could come to your defense. When you do see her again, she finds out you're in a MC, and not the kind that rides bikes on the weekends with friends." She pauses and arches her brow. "Why would she trust anything about you at that point?"

"She's never been in danger with me. I'm nothing like her asshole ex."

"No one is saying you are, sweetheart, but when you live like that—in fear every morning when you wake up because you're scared to enrage the person sleeping next to you—it changes something in you. Not only does she not trust men in general, but she doesn't trust herself. People like her ex tell you over and over again the reason they act like that, the reason they hurt you is because you did something wrong. You're the problem, not them. How can she trust you enough to open up when she can't trust herself not to fall into a situation with another man like the one she ran from?"

It makes sense, the way my mom puts it.

"How did you know you could trust Trick?"

"Oh, it wasn't easy." My mom laughs and shakes her head. "And I made him work for it. I think for me, it was seeing him with you boys. Do you remember when you were playing baseball in the backyard with Ozzy and Knox? You hit that ball so hard, it came right through the slider." She points to the glass door that leads out into the yard.

"We were sitting in the living room watching a game and heard a huge crash. Trick jumped up and was so scared that something happened to one of you boys. He saw how scared you were. If we had been in Nebraska with your father, that would have sent him into a rage. But Trick? Once he saw no one was hurt, he was so impressed with your swing, he insisted I sign you up for baseball and he went to all your games. The only thing he asked was for you to practice farther away from the house."

I remember that day. God, I remember being so scared that he was going to fly off the handle.

"When I saw how Trick encouraged you, even after breaking the window, which wasn't cheap to replace, by the way, instead of getting pissed, I knew he would never hurt you or Knox. Or me, for that matter. Gramps and Trick thought for sure you would be a power hitting baseball player." She smiles at the memory.

"I only played one season."

"Yeah, Trick didn't care much for the coach or some of the other dads. That's one of the reasons why when Knox and Ozzy started playing football, he supported you in changing sports, too. Did I ever tell you he paid for every single season?"

I shake my head.

"Yup. I was a single mom, and you two were eating me out of house and home." She laughs. "Trick made sure you had everything you needed."

"Why didn't you ever tell me that?"

"Well, at the time, he didn't even want me to know. Janine said she and Gramps wanted to 'sponsor' young talent. But before Janine died, she told me a lot about what Trick did for us through the years. He didn't want me to think I owed him something I wasn't willing to give freely."

After everything my mom went through with my father, I'm so fucking glad we landed in Shine. I don't know how our lives would have turned out if she had decided to stick it out in Nebraska.

"Thanks, Mom." I stand and bend down to kiss her cheek. "I'm sure as shit happy you found your white knight."

"Oh, honey, he's far from that, but he's a good man. And he had a hand in raising three other good men."

Getting back on my bike to head to the clubhouse, my mom's words run through my head. Am I a good man? I'd like to think so. I may not follow the law in the traditional sense, but I follow the laws of loyalty and brotherhood. That's more important to me than any penal code.

I will always protect my family, and Charlie needs to understand in no uncertain terms that she's family. Shit, she's more than that. Now, I have to figure out how much more.

CHAPTER SIXTEEN
CHARLIE

What have I done? I basically just compared Linc to my abusive ex because he lives his life on the other side of the law. I didn't have faith in a man who's showed me nothing but kindness. A man who would burn his world down to protect a nineteen-year-old girl he met once in a diner, then found broken and bloody on the side of the road. That's not a man who would turn his back on me or turn me over to my abuser for knowing a few details about his club and their less-than-legal dealings.

This man, this club, protects women. Ozzy could have retaliated against Stacia for running her mouth. If any of these men were like my ex, they would have raised a hand to her and never felt a moment of regret, but no one did. Sure, he kicked her out, but that was because she was causing problems. He didn't beat her to hell for disrespecting him or the club.

"You okay?" Lucy asks as I listen to Linc's bike roar away from the clubhouse.

I shake my head. "No."

She pulls me in for a hug. "Honey, you guys will figure this out. Once he gets back, you two can talk."

"He's never been anything but kind to me, but I was so messed up from what Jace did that I couldn't see past my fear."

And now, before I had enough time to confide in him about what I'd taken from Jace and why we were in this mess, he found out from someone else. That had to have hurt. Instead of me being open with him, he found out I was keeping secrets. Instead of building something on trust and respect, he thinks I don't trust him. For a man like him, that goes hand in hand with respect.

"Charlie," Ozzy calls in his deep voice. "A word." He nods toward his office.

"Do you want me to go with you?"

God bless Lucy, but it's time I start standing on my own two feet. Plus, he didn't ask to speak to her, and if there was ever a time *not* to piss off the MC president, now would be it.

"No, I'll be fine." I give her a weak smile. She doesn't buy it for a second, not that I imagined she would.

Walking into his office feels like getting called to see the principal—if the principal was an MC president who had a way of looking at you that made you want to tell him every secret you ever had. What I don't expect is for it to be so tidy in here. Everything has its place, and I can tell he's been working on paperwork from the reading glasses placed on a stack. Huh. I don't know why seeing those humanizes the intimidating man behind the desk, but it does.

"Linc told you we know what you have."

"Yes, sir."

Ozzy shoots me a wry smile. "No need to be formal, sweetheart. I just want to hear it from you." He gestures toward the chair in front of his desk, and I take a seat.

"That night, when Linc was arrested, I didn't really know what I took. I mean, I knew it was important to Jace, and it held some kind of evidence for something, but I didn't know what exactly. I swear to you, I didn't know the club was involved for sure until today."

"But you had suspicions?"

I bite my lip, scared to be honest, but there's no doubt in my mind Ozzy is the type of guy to see through lies.

"I did. He didn't use your guys' names, but he used initials. When Linc knew who Cillian Doyle was, I figured you had dealings with them. That's why I didn't say anything. I was afraid if anyone knew I had information on the Irish mafia, I would be turned over to them or something."

Ozzy nods as I continue.

"I was scared. That's my reason. The only thing I knew about Cillian was he's related to Jace. The idea that he was anything like Jace scared the shit out of me. I thought if he ever found me, it would make my time with my ex look like child's play."

"You don't have a very high opinion of most men, do you?" He tilts his head to the side and studies me. There's sadness in his voice that surprises me.

"I haven't met too many good ones." It's sad, but it's my truth.

"Charlie, we aren't going to hurt you or turn you over to the Irish or the Italians."

"The Italians?"

Ozzy nods, irritation crossing his face. "Seems your ex made a deal with them. You and Linc for the notebook."

I'm stunned speechless. "Why does he want Linc? This has nothing to do with him."

He shakes his head. "This has everything to do with him. He's the one who made it possible for you to run with that notebook. Your ex has a big score to settle with him because of what Linc did to him. Looks to me like he's been biding his time, hoping to kill two birds with one stone. That the two birds are together probably has him thinking his job will be easier."

"But why go to the Italians? His cousin is in the Irish mob." I don't know the inner workings of the mafia, but that seems like something that would be seriously frowned upon.

"Cillian's boss said Jace hasn't done any jobs for him for quite some time. He was getting into the product he was moving for his cousin. Being blood meant he wasn't put down, but they knew they couldn't trust him, so they cut him off. He's lucky it didn't cost him his life, but the stupid fuck doesn't see it that way."

"Makes sense. Jace always thought he was entitled to things that weren't his."

A dark cloud passes over Ozzy's face. "That doesn't happen here, and we don't stand for that. Ever. You may have never known any man worth a shit, and I can't tell you to believe the men in this club are. That depends on your idea of what a good man is. But I can tell you, not a man in my club or associated with my club would ever hurt a woman. If they did, they would answer to me, and I'm a firm believer in an eye for an eye."

I hear the conviction in his voice, and the fact that his violent words bring me comfort surprises me. In a clubhouse full of men who live by their own rules in a brutal world, I feel safe. That's certainly never something I thought I'd believe.

"Another reason the Irish decided not to get involved was because I assured them I would handle the situation. That means I need the notebook. That's all the Irish care about. Well, that and finding Jace. He's not only a threat to you but to their operations now. He crossed a line, and they want blood."

"Okay," I concede. "It's with my things." I stand and head to the door.

"All this other shit, we'll figure out. Linc's a good man. He just needed a minute to cool off."

My eyes are downcast as I blow out a nervous breath. "I hope you're right."

After returning with the notebook, Ozzy dismisses me, obviously stressed over the situation. Since Linc's gone and it's been a hell of a morning, I decide to lie down in my bed and attempt to decompress from everything that's happened the last few days. It's been a whirlwind, and I'm in desperate need of a reset. Lucy is there waiting for me, so my plan to rest and think is out the window.

"What did Ozzy have to say," she asks, sitting up in bed.

"I gave him the notebook. He said it's not only Jace that's after me." I fill her in on what Ozzy told me, not just about the Italians, but about the club and how they don't put up with any man abusing women.

"That tracks. I've never gotten the feeling that we weren't safe with these guys. Not like other clubs."

Before I can question her about what she means or how she would know anything about other clubs, there's a knock on the door.

Linc pops his head in. "Hey, Charlie girl. Ozzy wants to see us in his office."

There's no anger in his tone, not like when he left, but there is a certain resignation I don't like hearing.

"Okay."

When I move to pass him through the doorway, he grabs my hand, stopping me.

"I'm sorry."

It's a simple apology, but no one has ever said those words to me and meant them. Not like I know Linc does.

Brushing my lips against his for a brief moment, I pull away with a soft smile.

"Let's go talk to Ozzy."

When we get to Ozzy's office, Jude is waiting there for us. Linc gives him a questioning look. Jude shrugs, just as confused about why he's been summoned for this meeting as well.

"I looked through the notebook Charlie had," Ozzy begins. "That fucker collected information about routes to Canada and Mexico. He wrote down locations and coordinates for Irish safe houses and also kept track of some runs we handled for them. Some of it's in code, only using initials, but I recognized a lot of it since I was there. If this got into the hands of those Italian fuckers, it would compromise not only the Irish but us as well."

Ozzy leans back in his chair and steeples his fingers.

"I spoke with Finn. He wants to see the book so he can figure out what and where he needs to make changes. Even though Jace doesn't have the notebook anymore, I don't doubt he remembers plenty."

"Seems perfectly reasonable. We've always had a good relationship with them. As long as they know Charlie isn't a part of this after handing the notebook over, I don't have a problem with it," Linc agrees.

"That's not all he said. They have reason to believe Jace is in town. He knows this is our town, so it makes sense he's come here to try to find an opportunity to take Charlie. Since he's after both of you,"—he points to Linc and me—"I want you guys to lie low somewhere until either us or the Irish deal with him. I'd like to keep it as far away from the clubhouse as possible. We don't need anybody coming in here and shooting the place up. The Italians have already done that, and I don't want another war with them if we can avoid it." He turns to Jude. "That's where you come in."

"What? I don't have some secret hideaway." Jude says, confused as to where he fits in all of this.

"Jace found you in Texas. Whether it was because he'd somehow tracked down Charlie or was after Linc, we can't be certain at this point. We also don't know the full extent of his knowledge about our club. There are too many variables I'm not sure of, so I don't want to send you to one of our safe houses only to have it compromised."

"Okay..." Jude says, still not following Ozzy's train of thought.

"Call your brother. I need a favor."

"Well, shite."

When Jude pulls out his phone, I quietly ask Linc who Jude's brother is.

"Ex-Royal Marine. Does undercover commando shit for pay these days. He has contacts all over the place and collects favors like a kid collects baseball cards."

When the call connects, Jude puts it on speaker.

"Little brother," I hear a heavily accented voice come through the line. "To what do I owe the pleasure? Are you calling me to wish me a happy birthday?"

"Your birthday isn't for another week."

"True, but I've decided I'm declaring it my birthday month, you know, like all the kids do these days."

"Those kids are twats," Jude replies.

"Too true." His brother laughs.

"I have you on speaker with Ozzy, Linc, and Linc's girl, Charlie."

"Hello, Liam," Ozzy says.

"Ozzy, you big lumbersnack, how the hell are you?"

"What the fuck is a lumbersnack?" Ozzy says with a disgusted look on his face.

"Just a bloke who wears flannels and has a beard. I heard it on that video app everyone has nowadays."

"I'm going to need you to never say that to me again." Ozzy is scowling at the phone in Jude's hand, and it takes everything in me to hold in my laughter.

"Sorry, you're a big bad biker, not a lumbersnack," Liam replies drily.

"Good God, can we please move on?" Jude has apparently had enough of his brother's needling.

"Sure, sure. What can I do for you, gentlemen?"

"Liam, I need a safe house for a few days," Ozzy says.

"Does this have to do with why my brother needed new wheels last week?"

"It does."

"And does it have something to do with Charlotte Saunders?"

"How do you know my full name?" I ask Jude's brother.

"Hello, darling," Liam greets. "It's my business to know a lot of things about a lot of people, especially the people my one and only brother surrounds himself with. After Texas, I did some digging. That ex of yours is turning out to be a real problem."

I sit back in my seat next to Linc, incredibly uncomfortable with how much this man seems to know about me.

"It's okay, Charlie, he's on our side." Linc's reassuring words do little to calm my anxiety about Liam.

"As for your request Ozzy, I have a little place I think will suit your needs. I keep it well stocked, if you catch my drift."

I shoot Linc a questioning look.

"He has some sort of arsenal in there," he whispers.

"I'll give my brother the particulars. When do they plan on being there?"

"They'll be leaving within the hour," Ozzy responds, looking at the three of us.

Linc nods in agreement.

"Alright then. Take me off speaker, little brother, and I'll give you the information you'll need to get there and get set up." Liam says. "Oh, and Ozzy? You know this means you owe me a favor now, correct?"

"I figured you wouldn't be doing this out of the kindness of your heart," Ozzy replies.

Liam laughs. "That's a luxury men like us can't afford. Cheerio," Liam says with fake enthusiasm before Jude takes him off speaker and finishes his call.

"My brother is a wanker," Jude mumbles, pocketing his phone.

"That may be true, but I feel better having you guys safe where no one will think to look. We know for certain Jace has no idea where any of Liam's safe houses are located. I'll deal with your brother if it means getting this shit handled."

"Thank you for helping me," I tell Ozzy.

"The second that piece of shit opened fire on my guys, he brought the club into it, sweetheart. If he thinks the Italians can keep him safe now, he's wrong."

The three of us stand to leave when Ozzy speaks again.

"I'll make it clear to the Italians that Jace's notebook isn't up for grabs, and unless they want a war with us *and* the Irish, they'll cut him loose and let us deal with him." Ozzy looks Linc in the eye. "Once we have him, I'll let you know."

Linc nods, and we leave the office.

Lucy is waiting nervously by the bar. As soon as she sees me emerge from the hallway, she runs over.

"What's going on?" she asks.

"We're taking off for a few days. Ozzy said he's going to take care of it, then we'll come back," I reply.

"Don't worry, love, you'll only miss me for a little while," Jude interjects.

"Oh, Jude," Lucy laughs like he's the biggest idiot on the planet. "If you think I'm not going with Charlie, you seriously need to have your head examined." She turns her attention back to me. "So, where to, sister?"

Jude lets out a low growl. "Bollocks."

CHAPTER SEVENTEEN
UNC

There's a soft knock on my door as I pack a bag.

"Yeah," I call.

The door opens, and Charlie peeks her head in with a small, apprehensive smile gracing her lips.

"Hey," she says in a quiet voice. "Mind if we talk for a minute?"

I tilt my head, and she enters the room, sitting on my bed that's still in disarray from the night we spent tangled in my sheets.

We haven't really talked since I stormed out of the clubhouse this morning. The ride cleared my head, but as soon as I got back, it's been one thing after another. I know we need to have a serious discussion about everything going on and where the idea of us falls in the middle of it.

Charlie isn't meeting my eyes as I lean against my dresser, waiting for her to speak. Instead, she sits quietly, nervously picking at her nails. I hate seeing her like this. This is the nervous girl I met six years ago who was afraid of her own shadow, not the woman I've gotten to know.

"I'm sorry," she says, finally meeting my gaze. "I should have told you what I stole from Jace. Honestly, I was going to this morning. The truth is everything the last few days has felt like a dream, and I didn't want to face reality."

"What do you think reality would have looked like?"

She shakes her head and lets out a deep sigh. "I knew back in Texas the book had information on your friends. The idea that you would be loyal to them like you are with your brothers went through my mind more than once."

"You mean the Irish?"

"Yeah. At the bar, you knew who they were, and it seemed like, at the very least, you and the club were in business with them. There I was, this girl you barely knew who had all this information that could hurt them. The idea you would do something to me or Lucy because of what I knew scared the shit out of me."

"Charlie, the Irish are business associates, not friends. If I thought for a second they would have been any danger to you, Ozzy never would have told them you were here. They aren't like the Italians or your ex. No one here is."

"I see that now, but you have to understand, Linc, never, and I mean never, has anyone protected me. The last couple years I spent with Jace, everyone and everything came before me. If one of his slimy friends flirted with me, it was my fault for 'throwing myself at them.'" She uses air quotes as though it was something she often heard from that monster. "The idea you would have reacted the same way kept me silent. But getting to know you and your brothers better, I realized this morning how dumb that was."

"Damn straight," I tell her. "We protect the people important to us, not throw them to the wolves."

"I was scared you would have turned me over to them," she says quietly.

I move to sit next to her and brush her dark locks away from her face.

"Look at me, Charlie." her sad eyes turn in my direction. "I would never in a million years do that. I'm not your ex. I don't get off on hurting women. There is nothing more important to me and this club than protecting the people we care about. If the Irish had a problem with that, you can bet your perfect ass, we would be the ones standing in front of you." I can't control the urge to lean in and kiss her enticing pout. When I pull away, I continue. "We aren't perfect men, and we live by our own laws, but we aren't scumbags, and we don't do business with scumbags."

"You're the first man I've ever felt safe with. I guess I was afraid that feeling was all in my head."

"The only thing that was all in your head was the idea I would have ever done anything to hurt you or ever let anyone else hurt you. I'm not built that way." I press my forehead to hers. "But, babe, you have to trust me. If you can't trust me, then I can't trust you to be honest with me, even when it scares you. Even if you think I'll be the only man standing in front of you. I will always put you and your safety first... no matter what."

"I can do that. With anyone else I don't think I'd be able to, but with you, I know I can." Charlie takes my hand and links our fingers.

"Well, good thing you don't have to worry about anyone else." I give her a half-smile. "This is it for me, Charlie. I didn't think I'd ever see you again. The only thing I hoped was you were out in the world living a happy life, and that was good enough for me. I was content with my status quo, but now that you're here with me, in my bed and in my life, there's no going back to how things were without you. You've taken something from me, and I'll be damned if you ever give it back." I put her hand over my heart and the sweetest smile I've ever seen in my life graces her full lips.

A loud knock bangs on my bedroom door.

"Are you done packing?" Jude asks. "We need to get on the road."

Leave it to my prick of a best friend to ruin this moment.

"Yeah," I yell back.

Twisting around to face Charlie again, I give her a quick kiss on the mouth and stand from the bed.

"Ready, Charlie pie?"

She rolls her eyes and lets out a little giggle. "Oh Jesus, here we go. When are you going to give up?"

"Never."

The ride to Liam's safehouse is uneventful. The only problem we've had so far was before we left the clubhouse. Lucy was the opposite of excited about having to ride on the back of Jude's bike.

"Seriously. Why can't we take a car?" she asked the group standing around the bikes, waiting for her to get on.

"Because our bikes are faster. I don't want to be stuck in traffic." Jude replied. "Plus, I don't want to. Get on the bike, Lucifer."

She squints her eyes and starts counting backward from a hundred.

"Fine," she concedes when she gets to seventy-three.

"Believe me, this is as much a pain in my ass as it is yours." Jude handed her a helmet, which she put on with jerky movements.

Charlie laughed quietly behind me, wrapping her arms tightly around my middle. Ozzy came up next to me before I fired up the engine.

"Any sign of trouble, get safe. There's no reason to play the hero this time. We got it handled on this end, brother."

Ozzy and I talked about what I'd like to see happen when they finally find that piece of shit. The dumb fuck has no idea what he started when he took shots at us in

Texas. He'll soon realize, though, and I'll be the one to make sure he never forgets.

When we get to the small cabin, Charlie hops off my bike and does an adorable little spin.

"It's so pretty here. I almost feel like we're on vacation or something."

Walking up behind her, I put my arms around her waist and kiss the crown of her head.

"It is, babe. Just in a super-secret fortified safe house."

She laughs. "Yeah, totally the same thing."

"Smartass." I smack her on her perfectly round ass.

Her giggle loosens the knot in my chest. A few days here and we won't have to worry about Jace or the Italians again. My brothers are handling it back in Shine, and I get to spend some time with my girl.

Lucy walks over to us and looks at the cabin. "God, if I didn't know better, I'd think you brought us to a murder cabin in the middle of nowhere."

"I fucking wish," Jude mumbles as he walks past and heads to the front door.

"I simply can't tell you how excited I am to get to spend however many days with that absolute ray of sunshine," Lucy says, sarcasm dripping from every syllable.

We trudge up the stairs, our limbs a little stiff from the last few hours of riding. Usually, a ride like that wouldn't bother me in the least, but I was tense from keeping an eye out for any signs of Jace or the Italians.

It'll be nice to relax somewhere safe with my girl next to me.

"Okay, kids, here's how it works. There's a keypad at every door and sensors on all the windows. When you enter the house, you have twenty seconds to turn off the alarm."

"What happens after twenty seconds?" Lucy asks.

"You don't want to know," Jude replies menacingly.

Lucy rolls her eyes, completely unaffected by his implied threat.

"We're totally off the grid, so it's generators and firelight from here on out. There's no cell service, either. According to Liam, you can track just about anyone through their phone."

Sounds on par with what I know of Jude's brother.

We step into the cabin, and Jude shows us the code and how to set the alarm once we're inside.

Taking a look around the space, it really isn't much.

"Your brother's a minimalist?" Lucy asks.

It's what you would expect of a cabin in the middle of the woods. A couch that's probably been here about as long as the cabin, with an old worn-in recliner next to it. There's a fireplace covering one wall without anything on the mantle. The appliances in the kitchen are also old as shit. I open the small fridge and thankfully cold air blasts me in the face. At least that works. It looks like someone even stocked it for us.

Eying the steaks, I pull one out and show Jude. "That was nice of your brother."

He shakes his head. "One of his buddies was out here with his old lady. Liam told them he needed it for a job, so they had to find somewhere else. I guess she tends to have a hard time being around a lot of people, so they use the cabin to get away from the city."

"Good for us then. We have plenty of shit to grill while we're here."

When I walk back into the living room both of the bedroom doors are open. I peek my head in one and find Charlie putting our stuff away in the closet. The simple gesture of taking care of me puts a smile on my face.

"Hey, babe. Did you happen to pack a swimsuit?"

Charlie looks at me like I've lost my mind. "Why on earth would I have thought to do that?"

"Don't worry, I brought a couple," I hear Lucy call from the room next door. I knew I liked this girl.

"Why?" Charlie replies.

Lucy walks to the doorway and leans against it. "Why not? Since no one would tell me where we were going, I figured I'd pack a little of everything. For all I knew, we could have been hiding out in some palatial estate with an indoor pool or some shit. Seemed like a good idea to be prepared for anything."

"You wish, princess," Jude calls from the couch.

"You have no idea just how far off you are with the princess remark, biker boy."

"Whatever you say," he replies as he heaves himself off the couch. "Linc, let's go to the basement, so I can show you where my brother keeps..." He looks between the girls. "Some of his things."

Lucy rolls her eyes. "If you mean his personal arsenal, I figured he had one." She taps her finger against her chin. "Unless it's some secret red room of pleasure. Then I'm not sure you should be spilling your brother's secrets."

Jude stares at Lucy, giving her a deadpan glare. "Do you ever stop?"

"Nope," she replies, popping the P.

"Come on." Jude jerks his head, and I follow him down the narrow staircase.

The basement is cut short by a wall with a steel door that has a keypad next to it. Jude enters the same code used for the security system, and the door unlocks. Inside are rows of guns, about the same amount that we keep at the clubhouse. Below the weapons are the ammunition used for each one.

I let out a low whistle. "This is far from the red room Lucy was talking about."

"Quite," Jude replies. "I have to ask you something, and I don't want you to get angry about it."

"Okay," I reply, drawing out the word.

"Are you okay being tucked away here while the other brothers take care of this mess with Jace?"

I mull over his question while staring at Liam's arsenal.

"I don't love the idea, no, but Ozzy says he has it handled, and I trust him to do what's best for the club.

You weren't there when the Italians attacked the club-house. For weeks, everyone was watching their back. We had to go on lockdown until it was sorted. Ozzy's girlfriend at the time got shot. He's never had to deal with anything like that as prez, so I understand his hesitancy to throw us into an all-out war." I shrug my shoulders. "I don't know, man. It's hard to feel like I should be helping the brothers catch this guy, but at the same time, I want to make sure Charlie's safe. What better place than somewhere Jace or the Italians won't know to look?"

"I get you, mate. If I had a woman in trouble, I'd want her as far away as possible, too."

"What about you, though?" I ask Jude, considering he's on a glorified babysitting job he didn't ask for.

"Someone has to keep you kids in line. Who knows who could catch you unawares while you're busy between the sheets with your girl? Plus, I could use a little time away. Since Charlie came around, the bunnies have been in a tizzy. I'm tired of the drama." Jude sends me a smirk.

"I'm sorry," I drawl. "Is my woman being here making it hard to get your dick sucked?"

"All any of them want to do is complain about having those two there and not having to earn their keep. It's hard to get sucked off when their damn mouths won't stop yapping."

"Never let it be said that you aren't a sensitive soul, my friend."

"Trust me, mate," Jude smirks. "That will never be said."

Jude and I have had each other's backs for years. There's no doubt in my mind him being here is more than needing to get away from the bunny drama. Aside from Knox, my actual brother by blood, there's no one I trust more with my life and, by extension, Charlie's.

"You guys want to head to the lake before it gets dark?" I hear Charlie call down the stairs.

"Be right up, Charlie pie."

"Ugh, try again." Though her voice may sound annoyed, I'd bet money there's a smile on my girl's face.

"We good here?" I ask Jude as we turn off the lights and head back upstairs.

"Right as rain, mate."

Jude clasps me on my back as we walk into the living room and find Charlie and Lucy ready for the lake.

When I see Charlie in a bright red bikini, which is probably at least one size too small, I nearly go weak in the fucking knees.

"See, good thing I'm here. There's no way you won't be distracted," Jude remarks next to me.

I shove my friend a little harder than necessary, because fuck him for noticing, and he laughs.

"My brother probably has something that will pass as swim trunks somewhere. I'll sort it while you guys rustle up some beers and snacks to take with us."

I raise a finger and beckon Charlie to me while Lucy makes herself busy swiping sunscreen all over herself.

When Charlie's within reach, my arm bands around her waist and pulls her flush against my front.

"Goddamn, baby, seeing you in that little getup is making me think thoughts that have nothing to do with going to a lake." I nuzzle the side of her neck and growl. "Do you have any idea what I would give to have you all to myself right now?"

Charlie presses closer to me, feeling the evidence of my arousal against her bare stomach.

"I have some idea."

Jude comes from one of the rooms and throws a pair of trunks at my head.

"Hey, Lucifer, I would have thought you didn't need all that sunscreen seeing as you're from the depths of hell. Figured you would be immune from a little burn."

"Fuck you, you pasty British slag."

Jude's eyes widen. "Kitty has claws."

"Hold on to those thoughts. I'm afraid of what'll happen if we leave these two unsupervised," Charlie says, reaching up and kissing my cheek.

Leave it to Jude to cockblock me at every turn.

CHAPTER EIGHTEEN
UNC

"Mmmm," Charlie moans as I wake her up with my tongue between her legs. Yesterday at the lake, she was doing everything in her power to tempt me in that little red bikini. I got my payback, though. Instead of wringing every last orgasm from her like I normally would, I edged her to within an inch of her sanity. Every time she was about to come on my tongue, I pulled back. Her cries of frustration fell on deaf ears. I eventually let her come on my cock—I'm not a monster after all—and I've never in my life experienced a pussy clench so tightly, I thought she was going to snap the fucking thing off.

"Are you teasing me again today," she groans.

Lifting my head from her center, I shoot her a salacious wink.

"That was yesterday, babe. Today I'm going to see how many times I can make you come before breakfast."

"I like this plan much better." Her hands run through my hair, scratching my scalp with her short nails. The touch sends shivers through my body before she pushes my head back down.

"Better get to work then," she says with a soft laugh.

"Yes, ma'am."

Taking my sweet time, I lick her from bottom to top, making sure to circle my tongue around her swollen clit the way she likes, if the way she tightens her fists in my hair is any indication. I fucking love having my head between my woman's thighs. The sounds she makes and her taste drive me wild. I've never had this reaction to a woman and can't imagine not doing this with her every fucking day. When I look up from the most perfect pussy I've ever had the pleasure of tasting, Charlie's neck is arched, her head thrown back as she bites her bottom lip.

"Feel good, baby?"

"God, yes," she breathes out.

My fingers circle her clit while I lick round her opening before delving my tongue inside her. I want to taste everything I do to her. Instead of making her wait like I did last night, I replace my tongue with my fingers inside her tight channel and begin pumping, making sure to graze the spot inside that is sure to have her coming hard and fast. My tongue goes back to her clit, flicking it over and over as I fuck her with my fingers.

Only moments later, she's biting the pillow as her orgasm rolls through her, soaking my hand. As she comes down from her high, I make sure to lap up every creamy drop. Goddamn, this is the mother fucking breakfast of champions.

Charlie's breaths begin to slow as I make my way up her tan body. Being in the sun has given her skin that summer glow and the little lines from her bikini bottoms around her hips are too tantalizing not to run my tongue over. She giggles and squirms as I move my mouth from one hip to the other, making sure to taste every inch of skin between.

"Linc, I need you inside me," she moans when I get to her delectable nipples and work them into tight buds with my lips and tongue.

"Patience baby. I'm just getting my full. You don't want to leave your man starving, do you?"

Her eyes roll, even though I know she loves the torture.

"I thought you were going to be nice today and not make me wait."

Deciding I tortured her enough yesterday, my hand goes from the nipple I was pinching to the nightstand. I release her other nipple with a pop and rise to my knees.

"God, there's nothing like seeing you flushed from the orgasm I just gave you and begging for more," I say, running my hand over the blush covering her body. "You're fucking beautiful, Charlie."

Freeing the condom from its wrapper, I slide the latex over my rock-hard cock. When I line up at her entrance, my gaze locks with her blue eyes, begging me to fill her. I push in and watch her eyes go half-mast, both of us letting out a deep moan. There aren't many absolutes in my life, but one thing I know for certain is I will never stop craving this woman.

My body falls over hers, and I rest the bulk of my weight on my forearms, locking eyes with Charlie as I move in and out of her in slow, deliberate thrusts. I want her to feel me for days just like I feel every part of her even when we aren't connected like this. She's burrowed into my soul in a way I've never felt before, and I wouldn't change a damn thing.

Charlie doesn't take her eyes off me as her walls tighten around my shaft, as though neither of us can look away from the other. This moment is tethering us together, and to look away would break the soul-deep connection that seems to have snapped into place.

When she falls over the edge, I'm right there with her. I lean down and take her mouth in a kiss that seals whatever new promise we made with our bodies. Our foreheads press together, and as though she's reading my mind, she whispers, "I felt it, too."

I don't need to explain or ask any questions. I know exactly what she's talking about. Instead of being scared or confused, I relish this new place we've found ourselves in. This is it. Charlie is mine, and there's no way, come hell or high water, anything will ever change that fact.

When we dress for the day, my hands can't seem to stay off her body.

"They're going to think you're keeping me here as some sort of sex slave if we don't show our faces at some point today," Charlie says, laughing as I nuzzle that spot behind her ear that drives her wild.

"I don't care. Let them think what they want. Isn't this supposed to be some kind of vacation or something?"

"If you consider hiding from the mafia and a crazy ex a vacation, then sure."

"I'll gladly take any alone time with you and call it whatever I want. Besides, I'm confident I can make you come at least twice more before we go out there."

Charlie laughs and throws her arms around my neck.

"I'm sure you could, but I think four before breakfast is enough to tide us both over for a little while."

After the most intense sex I'd ever had in my life, I had Charlie on all fours while I ate that sweet cunt from behind before driving deep inside her again. Fuck, remembering how my cock looked sliding in and out of her while wetness ran down her thighs is making things tight in my jeans again. I hold her tighter to my body so she can feel what she's doing to me. Grabbing the back of her head, my mouth latches on to hers, kissing her deeply, needing her to understand that it will never be enough. No matter how many times we kiss or how many times I'm inside her, I'll never get enough.

Her stomach rumbles, and she giggles, breaking the kiss.

"Okay, okay... let's show Lucy and Jude signs of life and get you fed."

"Sorry," Charlie says as she straightens her clothes.

"Never be sorry, babe." I bend and give her a quick kiss. "I love watching you eat all the meat," I say, remembering when she blurted that out in the little diner when we were heading back to Shine from Texas.

"Oh my God, I was so nervous sitting next to you. I can't believe that came out of my mouth." Charlie covers her face with her hands in embarrassment.

Taking her hands in mine, I remove them and smile at her rosy cheeks.

"I thought it was adorable." I kiss the tip of her nose. "You're fucking adorable. I decided right then and there, I'd give you all the meat you could handle." I throw her a wink and smile playfully.

She lets out a noise between a laugh and a growl, smacking my chest. "Perv."

When I open the bedroom door to head to the kitchen, arguing is the first thing I hear.

"What the hell are you doing, woman? You don't bake bacon. You fry it. Everyone knows that."

"Listen here, you British asshole. Let's leave the cooking to people who actually like their food to have flavor. Not that bland shit you try to pass off as anything other than paste."

As we walk into the kitchen, the two loudmouths are standing in the middle of it with a baking tray between them, each trying to pull it out of the other's grasp.

"She's right," Charlie chimes in from beside me. "It really is easier and tastes better the way Lucy does it."

Jude gives Charlie a skeptical look but begrudgingly concedes, letting go of the pan.

"Fine," he grouses. "Let her ruin breakfast."

I chuckle as Jude walks past me and pat him on the shoulder. "Sometimes you just have to pick your battles, bud."

He stops and stares at me for a moment. "Everything with that one is a battle," he says, tilting his head toward the kitchen.

"It's not like you don't egg her on."

"I know. There's just something about her. It's like something in me refuses to let her win."

I don't bother telling him she beats him at every turn. Shooting, poker, and now cooking. If anyone asked me, I'd say he likes the challenge, not that he'd ever admit it.

Watching Charlie and Lucy in the kitchen laughing and cooking has me thinking about having this every day. Now that the truth about what she was hiding and why isn't a secret anymore, it's like this boulder she had sitting on her shoulder has disappeared. We aren't out of the woods yet, but these last two days, seeing laughter come easier and smiles coming more naturally makes me realize how heavy everything was weighing her down.

When this mess is taken care of, I'm not wasting any time. I want her in my bed every night, wearing my patch, and living in my house. Granted, I've been living at the clubhouse since I got back, but I want us to find a place of our own, away from any bunny drama and the late nights of partying. I want more mornings like this one.

After breakfast, with all of us stuffed beyond capacity, Charlie and I go back to our room and lie down. I'm on my back with Charlie draped over me, my arm resting on her waist.

"I love this," she mumbles sleepily.

For the first time in my life, the stillness doesn't make me uneasy or bored. I'm content being able to lie with her in my arms and daydream about the life we have ahead of us.

"Last one in is a rotten Englishman with a pasty complexion," Lucy calls, running for the dock.

Charlie laughs, giving Jude a not-so-apologetic look before she kisses me and runs after her friend.

There's nothing much to do around here, so we're making it a lake day again. Any day I get to see my girl in that fuck-hot red bikini is a win, so I don't mind another lazy day drinking beers and lounging by the water.

"Have you heard anything from your brother?" I ask Jude after we situate ourselves on the beach chairs.

With no cell reception, I didn't expect much contact. Of course, Liam gave Jude a satellite phone for emergencies, but the thing hasn't gone off once.

"No, but I figure no news is good news."

Liam, being the cagey asshole that he is, told Ozzy if anything were to happen on the Jace or Italian front to call him, and he would get in touch with Jude. Ozzy didn't like the idea of not being able to talk to his men any time he needed, instead having to use Liam as the go-between, but what could we do? Liam's house, Liam's rules.

"He really wants to make sure no one knows about this place, huh?"

"It's his personal safe house, so yeah. If he ever has to lie low, he needs to make sure it's one hundred percent off the grid with only a select few even knowing it exists, let alone where it is."

Looking over the small lake, I see Charlie emerging from the water like a goddess, all that wet skin and gorgeous curves with those tiny ties on her bottoms just begging to be loosened by my teeth. Shit, these shorts don't do shit to hide my rapidly hardening length.

When she reaches me, I grab her hand and pull her on top of me. Charlie laughs and leans down for a kiss.

"I'm getting you all wet," she says as I run my nose along the column of her throat.

"I don't mind a bit," I reply, biting her earlobe.

She giggles and sits up to reach into the cooler for a beer.

"Shit, we're out. I'll run up and grab a few."

"Here, take my seat. I'll go," I say as I begin to move her off me.

"No, it's okay. I'll be right back." She smacks a loud kiss on my lips and hops off my lap.

I turn and watch her biteable ass as she makes her way to the cabin.

"You're in love with her," Jude comments from next to me.

If he thought his observation would shock or surprise me, he's wrong. When Charlie and I made love this morning, I felt her deep in my bones. I didn't try to deny it to myself then, and I'm certainly not going to deny it now.

"Yup. And when we get back, I'm going to make her my old lady," I reply with a confident smirk.

Jude doesn't say anything else, just nods and looks back over the water.

"Where'd Charlie go?" Lucy asks, casting a shadow over Jude.

"You're blocking my sun, Lucifer."

"Oh, I'm so sorry, your highness. I didn't realize you owned the damn sun." She doesn't move.

"She went to grab more beers."

I look behind me and expect to see her coming back, but there's nothing but silence.

"I'll go check on her." Hopefully, I can catch her before she comes back. She's been tempting me all afternoon in her suit. I wouldn't mind moving the bottoms out of the way and sinking deep inside her before we come back with beers. Besides, who knows how long Lucy and

Jude will be busy bickering. I doubt they'd even notice we're gone.

Walking up the stairs, I call out to Charlie. "Babe, there's a little problem I need your help with," I say, referring to the growing erection in my shorts. "Okay, maybe little isn't the right word." I open the door and stop dead in my tracks, the blood draining from my face.

Jace has Charlie by the hair, and he's injecting something into her neck. Her face is bloody, and her right eye is swollen almost completely shut.

"You motherfucker," I yell as I charge toward him. Before I've barely made it two steps inside the cabin, Jace lets go of Charlie's hair, grabs a gun, and shoots me, the bullet tearing through my gut and knocking me back off my feet. I grab my side and watch as Charlie's blank eyes stare at me, unseeing and about to close. The pain is almost unbearable as I try to move toward my woman.

"Uh-uh," Jace sneers as he watches my pathetic attempt to get to Charlie. I hear gunshots in the distance toward the lake.

"You're done. You and your friend. Did you really think you were going to keep what's mine?" Jace asks, kneeling next to me.

I'm losing too much blood too fast, causing my vision to go hazy along the edges.

"She doesn't have your notebook, you piece of shit." The words are disjointed and sound slurry to my own ears.

Jace looks back at Charlie. "Huh, well, that's too bad for her, but I'm still taking her, and there's nothing you can do about it."

Keeping my eyes open is a losing battle, and the last thing I see is Jace standing upright, his boot coming toward my face.

Then it's lights out.

CHAPTER NINETEEN
CHARLIE

The excruciating pain is the first thing that registers when I attempt to open my eyes. I manage to get one eye open, but the other won't budge. It's swollen shut. Son of a bitch, Jace hit me harder than I think he ever had. My head is fuzzy, and my mouth feels like I went on a three-day bender. Not that I ever have, but I imagine the complete lack of moisture and disgusting taste in my mouth would be similar.

Okay, Charlie, think. What happened?

I remember going up to the cabin to grab a few more beers. When I walked in, Jace was in there, sitting on the old recliner with a gun on his lap. Before I could turn and scream, he leapt off the chair and punched me in the face.

Explains the swollen eye.

I whirled around to fight him off, but he was moving so fast. He had me on my back with his fist tangled in my hair, then slammed my forehead on the hardwood floors. Fuck, that one hurt.

I remember feeling dazed when he wrenched my head back, then something pinching the side of my neck. Before whatever he injected in me took effect, Linc came in and charged Jace, but Jace was too fast and shot Linc.

Oh God. He shot Linc. Jude and Lucy had to have heard it. They were a good distance away at the lake, but there's no doubt in my mind they would have heard the loud gunshot.

That's all I remember before waking up here.

I take a look around my surroundings. My hands are zip-tied behind my back, and my ankles are duct taped to the metal folding chair in the middle of an old warehouse. I don't have any memory of getting here or anything that happened after Jace drugged me. I'm still in my bikini and chilled to the bone, but thankful for the small amount of coverage it provides—a very small amount.

"Oh good, you're awake. I was worried I gave you too much," Jace says, walking into my line of sight.

"What did you give me?" I croak.

"Just a little concoction my friends came up with. I guess they use it in their line of work."

"Is their line of work abducting women?"

"It is," he says matter-of-factly. "The Italians have done quite well for themselves in the skin trade. Boy, do they have a bone to pick with that motorcycle club you've been whoring yourself for."

Linc mentioned something about the Italians and the club not being on good terms for years, but he didn't say it had anything to do with them selling women.

"I don't have your book, Jace."

"Oh, I know. Your boyfriend told me that before I kicked him in the face."

I don't remember that part.

"Not that it matters. He was bleeding so much, I'm sure he's dead by now. You guys found a pretty remote place to hide from me."

It's remote, and no one except Liam knows where it is.

"How did you find us?" I ask.

"The day you were at the park. You didn't notice me when you were engrossed in whatever hand-to-hand combat you've learned since I last saw you. Hence the drugs. I put a teeny tiny little tracking device on his bike, courtesy of my new friends." Jace smiles like the sadistic asshole he is. "I've been keeping an eye on your boy since he got out of prison. That's how I found him in Texas. It was dumb luck I found you there, too. I knew my day would come, though. I figured he would eventually lead you to me."

So, Jace was after revenge on Linc in Texas, not me.

"Why? After all this time, Jace, why can't you just let me go?"

"Because," he says, kneeling down and grabbing my bruised face roughly. "You were mine. He thought he could beat me nearly to death, and you could just dis-appear?"

I try to move my face out of his hold, but he tightens his grip.

"That's not how this works. You took something from me and tried to run, but you should have known sooner or later I'd find you. Six years is a long time to imagine all the things I would do to you."

His gaze rolls down my front, and if the drugs didn't make me want to throw up whatever was in my stomach, the look he's giving me definitely would.

"Jace," I hear an unfamiliar accented voice call out.

My ex turns his attention to the four men that have entered the warehouse. All of them are dressed to the nines in three-piece suits and slicked-back hair. The man who called out Jace's name looks at me without so much as an ounce of interest or pity. The other three don't pay me any mind, either. Their lack of reaction does not bode well for me.

"Alberto, there you are. Glad you got my message," Jace says, standing from his crouched position in front of me, finally releasing my face.

The smile he gives the man is so at odds with how he was behaving toward me just moments ago. The bastard didn't even skip a beat going from hurting and threatening me to talking to whoever this Alberto guy is like they're long-lost buddies.

"This is the girl, then?" Alberto asks, coming over and studying me like I'm a prized heifer.

"Yeah, man, this is her."

"Where's this notebook you promised us?" Alberto asks as he circles around me.

"Well, that's the thing," Jace starts. "She doesn't have it. The dumb bitch gave it to Ozzy, so it's at the club-house. But I'm sure we can work something else out since you've been helping me."

What the fuck is Jace talking about, working something else out?

"That was not our deal. You were supposed to bring me the notebook, then we would pay you accordingly for the information. All you've brought me is a bruised-up girl and trouble from not only the Irish but the Black Roses."

"Right, yeah, but you know, sometimes things don't work out like we plan. I can't get you the notebook, but what about her?"

Umm, excuse me?

"I've heard you guys deal in more than blow and guns. You could get a pretty penny for her on the auction block, no?"

Alberto looks me over again, considering Jace's change of plan. It's not as if he has to imagine what's underneath any clothes I'm wearing, considering I'm still in this damn bikini.

After several tense moments, he nods. "Yes, she would do nicely, I think. What do you think, Luca?"

The other man looks at me with a lascivious grin that sends chills down my spine.

"We would make a pretty penny off her, boss."

Jace nods his head frantically as though this is the best idea he's ever had.

"There you go. With a little training from a strong hand, I'm sure she would fall in line. She always did for me," Jace says.

I'm going to be sick. The man who used to say he loved me not only nearly killed me on more than one occasion, but now he's selling me to these monsters.

"And what do you expect out of this new deal, Jace?" Alberto asks.

"Just a finder's fee. I understand if she isn't worth as much as what we originally agreed on, but I think something in the ballpark of ten thousand is fair, don't you?"

And that's what my life is worth to my ex.

"Fine, fine. Luca." He motions to the man, who reaches into his pocket and pulls out a thick wad of hundred-dollar bills.

Jace accepts the payment and comes over to the metal chair I'm sitting in, bending down to release my legs from their bindings.

"Don't try anything stupid, Charlie. These men won't be as forgiving as I've been."

"You call this forgiving, you sick piece of shit?"

"You're leaving with your life, aren't you?"

Does he honestly expect me to thank him for selling me into the skin trade instead of killing me?

Jace wraps his hand around my bicep and forcefully pulls me from the chair.

"Pleasure doing business with you," he tells Alberto.

Before he can hand me over, a metal door slams open, and three men walk in and open fire on the Italians. One goes down immediately while the other two dive behind pallets of cardboard. Alberto runs behind some wood pallets and returns fire.

"Did you sell us out, you fucking cunt? How the hell did the Irish know you were here?"

Alberto pops up and shoots at the three strangers, but the men have already found cover behind cement pillars scattered around the warehouse.

"I swear I didn't," Jace exclaims. He still has a tight hold of my arm as we crouch next to Alberto.

"I should have never made a deal with you in the first place. You've become more of a hassle than you're worth."

I think he's going to shoot Jace and probably me for his troubles, but instead, he pops up and fires at the Irish. Alberto gets off three rounds before crumpling to the floor, a bullet between his eyes. The other two Italians are still firing on the three Irishmen.

"We're getting the fuck out of here," Jace says, tightening his grip on me before making a run for the metal door only twenty feet from us.

We stumble through the door as the gunfire continues behind us. I hear shouts of "get the girl," but I can't tell if it's the Italians or the Irish, who I hope are here on Ozzy's behalf.

When the door slams behind us, I stumble and fall to the gravel lot. My knees scrape across the rocks when

Jace grabs me by the hair to drag me to a beat-up car I spot on the other side of the building. I catch my footing, and now that he isn't holding me by the arm, I lift my arms behind me, squeezing my elbows in and slamming them against my backside. The force of the action breaks the zip tie he had wrapped tightly around my wrist. Jace is so focused on getting to his car he doesn't notice at first. I claw at his wrist to try to dislodge his fingers from my hair.

He whirls around in a rage.

"Bitch," he yells, yanking me closer to him.

Perfect.

The movement causes me to slam into his chest. I reach around his back and grab the gun he has stashed in the waist of his jeans. He immediately feels what I've done and lets go of my hair, putting his hands in the air and taking a few steps back from me.

"Now, wait a second, Charlie. Let's talk about this. I have ten grand in my pocket—"

"Oh, the ten grand you took as payment for me?"

"I never would have let them take you. I was just trying to get some money so I could get far away. I swear I would have gotten you away from them before they even left the parking lot." Jace looks nervously between my face and the gun. "Come on. We can still get out of here. I'll take you back to Linc and even split the money with you."

"I saw you shoot him," I yell. "Do you honestly think I believe a single word you're saying? You don't give a shit about me, and you never have."

"I know I fucked up. I know I have a temper, but I'm willing to let it go, Charlie. I'll let you go if you just give me the gun. We'll get in the car right now, and I'll take you to Linc."

"Go fuck yourself, Jace."

"Listen, bitch, either the Italians or the Irish are gonna walk out of that door, neither of who you want to mess with. Give me the gun," he hollers.

He takes a step forward, and I take one back.

"You don't even know how to use that thing," he sneers as he keeps coming toward me.

I have a choice, and both scare the hell out of me. If the Irish are here, it's likely the MC knows where I am. God, what I wouldn't give for Linc to ride up on his bike and take care of this asshole in front of me. Since that's not going to happen, I can either hope it's the Irish who emerge from the warehouse and they're here to rescue me, or I can shoot this motherfucker and get the hell out of here.

"I said give me the fucking gun." He lunges for me, and I make my decision.

I pull the trigger, and Jace falls back on the gravel, blood oozing from beneath him. I stare at his prone body on the ground and lower the weapon.

Nothing happens.

I don't freak out or cry. Jace doesn't suddenly get back up and come after me like the nightmares I've had over and over again. Nothing happens—until I hear the rumble of motorcycles.

When I see the six motorcycles come to an abrupt halt in front of the warehouse, relief washes through me. Five of the bikers storm through the front door of the warehouse as Jude runs toward me. I'm still holding the gun on Jace, even though he hasn't moved. Jude walks past Jace's still form, taking a brief look at the motionless body.

"Hey, Charlie, It's okay. We're here."

He reaches out for the gun in my hand, and I release it from my death grip. When he secures it behind his back, my arm and the rest of my body begin to crumble to the ground.

"Woah, woah, I got you, sweetheart. You're alright."

Jude wraps me in his arms as my body begins to shake uncontrollably. That's when the tears come, big teardrops cascading down my cheeks. I couldn't control them if I tried, and being that it's all I can do to stay upright at the moment, I don't.

"Where's Linc?"

I catch Jude's stoic gaze that gives nothing away.

"Jude, where is he?" I refuse to believe that after everything we've gone through, everything we've endured, this is the end. I will not accept that Jace won in any way, shape, or form.

"He's alive, but he's not doing great. Last I checked he was still in surgery, but he's alive, Charlie."

The tears have turned into wracking sobs that take over my entire body.

"The Italians are taking care of," Ozzy says, walking up and surveying the scene. "You did good, sweetheart," he says, looking at Jace's body. Ozzy bends down and checks for a pulse. "Still alive but barely."

I don't know whether I should be glad I won't have his death on my conscience or upset my aim wasn't better.

"Come on, Charlie, I'm taking you to the hospital to get checked out. How you managed to hit him with one eye swollen shut is beyond me," Jude tells me. "Must have been my expert tutelage."

I huff out a hollow laugh. I appreciate him trying, but the only thing that will make me feel better is an update on Linc.

"God, I'm still in this stupid bikini," I remark as Jude herds me to a car that must belong to one of the Irish.

"Stay right there."

Yeah, like I'm going anywhere.

Jude jogs back from his bike with a change of clothes. I give the wad in his hand a questioning look.

"Did you really think Lucy would let me leave the cabin without something for you to change into?"

Oh my God, I didn't even think to ask about my best friend.

"Is she okay? All I remember is Jace shot Linc before whatever he injected me with knocked me out."

"She's perfectly fine. Worried out of her mind, but other than that, not a scratch. I'll let her tell you about it at the hospital."

Ozzy walks over to the car that must belong to one of the Irish as I'm changing in the back seat into a pair of soft shorts and a large t-shirt. From the smell of the shirt, I know it's Linc's. The tears come back full force as I wrap myself in his scent. Ozzy knocks on the window, and I roll it down.

"Jude is taking you to the hospital where Linc is. We're still a few hours outside of Shine. Lucy is waiting at the hospital, and Tanya is on her way up."

I nod and look at the warehouse. The Irish are standing outside having a smoke like nothing is amiss, even though there are dead Italians inside and one almost dead piece of shit a few yards from me.

"What about all this?" I ask, waving my hand in front of me.

"This..." Ozzy looks behind him. "Is nothing for you to worry about. We take care of family, sweetheart, and that's what you are now." Ozzy closes the door before Jude gets behind the wheel.

"Nice shirt," Jude comments.

I hold the neck to my nose, inhaling Linc's scent.

"Yeah."

God, please don't let this be the only thing I have left of him.

CHAPTER TWENTY
CHARLIE

The ride to the hospital is eerily quiet. Jude keeps looking from the rearview mirror back to the road over and over.

"Are you afraid more guys from the Italian crew are going to come after me?"

"I don't think we'll have to worry about them coming after us." He glances at me, then back at the road. "The Irish are cleaning up the mess. The Italians had a long-standing feud that involved us briefly, but Trick took care of it years ago. But the fact they were involved with anything having to do with us now has everyone a little on edge."

"What happened?"

"Before Linc or even Ozzy were in the MC, they came into the clubhouse and shot it up. They were unhappy with the business we were doing with the Irish and wanted to, I don't know, hurt the Irish or some such shite. Trick cut them down pretty quickly, and the head of the family and Trick had a tentative truce for the last decade and a half. Cataldi said it was a young capo trying to make a name for himself, and he understood that shooting up a clubhouse full of families and kids was crossing a line."

After the conversation involving Jace selling me to Alberto at the warehouse, I doubt there are many lines the Italians won't cross.

"Does Ozzy know they're in the business of selling women?"

Jude clenches his jaw and exhales. "There have been rumors, but considering we don't do any business with them, or anyone associated with them, it's just talk."

"Well, it's not. Jace was going to sell me to the men who got shot up. They're definitely in the skin trade."

"Trust me, Ozzy is going to be a part of whatever the Irish want to do to handle the Italians. No one that helped Jace in any of this bullshit is going to get away unscathed."

"What does that mean?"

"It means he's handling it, and you don't need to worry about it, sweetheart."

"It's kind of hard not to, considering where we just came from and where we're going, Jude." I'm being a little snippy, but I have zero fucks left to give.

"Listen, you don't know me, and up until a few days ago, I was afraid you were going to do something to screw my brother over. But believe me when I say Linc cares about you and that you're important to my brother, which means you're important to everyone in the club. We protect our own. If Linc wants you to know specifics, he has to make the call to tell you, but know that you're safe with us."

"Easier said than done," I mumble under my breath as we pull up to the ER.

Jude stays with me as the nurse hooks me up to the IV and tells me the doctor will be right in. Before she leaves, she makes sure to quietly let me know if I need to report the assault, she'll make sure no one else was in the room with me. Of course, she thinks the tense biker next to me did this to my face, if her suspicious glances at Jude are anything to go by.

I smile politely and thank her for her offer, but let her know there's no need. The story we came up with was I was mugged on my way to the car, and Jude was the good Samaritan who chased the attacker away.

I don't think she buys it.

After the doctor examines me, he confirms that nothing is broken and the swelling around my eye will go down in a few days, but to expect the bruising to take a bit longer. I don't bother telling him I'm used to dealing with the bruising and discomfort from being punched, worried the entire hospital will deem any biker in the building a woman beater I'm covering for. Nothing could be further from the truth.

"Do you have an update on Linc," I ask Jude for the millionth time.

"Not since the last time you asked fifteen minutes ago." Jude looks up from his phone and notices the hurt expression on my face. "Shit, Charlie. I'm sorry. That was rude as hell."

"It's okay," I tell him, even though my tone implies it was anything but.

He closes his eyes and inhales a deep breath, letting it out slowly through his nose.

"No, it wasn't," he says, looking at me with an apology swimming in his gaze. "There's a lot of shit going on with trying to clean all this up, and right now, we're right in the thick of it. I have no right to talk to you like that when you're as worried about your man as we all are."

"Thank you." I'm not used to men apologizing to me when they're in the wrong, so I'm not exactly sure how to handle the stressed-out biker.

The nurse comes back with my discharge paperwork as Jude gets a call from Ozzy.

"Oh, thank fucking Christ," he says into the phone before hanging up. "Linc's out of surgery and in a room. Not sure about visitors yet, but Ozzy said they'll let him know as soon as we can see him."

Relief flows through me. He made it out of surgery. Tears begin pouring out of my eyes again. If I was in a place emotionally to laugh at anything right now, the incredibly uncomfortable look on Jude's face as he awkwardly pats my back would have me in hysterics.

"This is good news. No need to cry, love."

"They're happy tears," I attempt to reassure him.

"Whatever you say." He tilts his head toward the thin curtain separating us from the rest of the ER. "Let's get out of here and meet up with the brothers that are here. Lucy is here, too. She's been texting nonstop since they would only let one person stay with you in the ER." I'd venture to guess the reason that person is Jude and not Lucy is because he knew Linc would give him hell for leaving me without protection.

Though Jude would never admit to being grateful for anything concerning Lucy, he's probably pretty happy he won't be the one to deal with my hysterical water-works anymore.

When we meet everyone in the waiting room, my best friend runs up to me, throwing her arms around me.

"Oh, thank God. You have no idea how scared I was when Jude and I went back to the cabin and found you gone and Linc bleeding on the floor. I've never been so terrified in my entire life." She walks us over to the plastic chairs and sits down, holding tightly to my hand the entire time.

"What happened at the lake?" I ask her.

"We heard the gunshot then a couple guys came out of the woods and started firing at us. It wasn't the same guys from Texas. I'd never seen these guys before."

"Were they in suits?" I ask, wondering just how in-volved the Italians were in all this.

"No, they looked like your run-of-the-mill scumbags. Jude grabbed me, and we took cover behind some trees. I honestly thought that was going to be it for me. Then we heard your ex shout they needed to go, and the guys ran toward the cabin. That's when I saw Jace carry you out. Jude started to take off after them, but they had ATVs or something. We didn't see them, but we heard them. He was too far away to catch up." Lucy's gaze holds an apology that is completely unnecessary.

"Hey," I say, squeezing her hand. "It's no one's fault except Jace's."

Lucy blows out a breath and continues her story. "When we got back to the cabin, Linc was unconscious on the floor. God, I was so scared he was dead. Jude ran over and checked his pulse, then called his brother. I guess one of the guys on his team was an army medic and was close by, so he was there minutes later. Liam called an ambulance for us, and we came straight here."

I'm so fucking thankful my best friend wasn't hurt and was able to get to Linc in time. God, this could have all turned out so differently.

Tanya and Trick come through the doors to the waiting room, frantically looking around for someone to give them answers. When she spots Ozzy, she runs to him, begging for information.

"He's stable, and they're setting him up in a room now. Let's find a nurse who can give us more information," he tells the distraught mother.

Tanya turns and sees me standing next to Lucy, who still hasn't let go of my hand.

"It'll be okay, sweetie. I can guarantee that boy has no intention of leaving you because of some bullet wound." The fact this woman is trying to console me while her son is just coming out of surgery that, let's face it, had it not been for me, he wouldn't have needed in the first place, leaves me speechless.

Tanya turns as she, Trick, and Ozzy go to talk to the woman at the nurses' station.

"This is all my fault," I say, collapsing back into the chair.

"Hey, now," Lucy says. "If I can't blame myself for not being able to get to you, then you can't blame yourself, either. You heard the doctors. He is going to be fine."

"Lucy, all I have ever done is bring trouble into his life. He lost six years of freedom because of me, and now he almost lost his life."

"Listen to yourself, Charlie. Did you not just tell me it was Jace's fault when I felt guilty for not being able to get to you before he took you? Why is it any different for you? You are, once again, taking responsibility for Jace's actions. Linc didn't go to prison because of you. He went because you were getting beat to hell by the man who should have protected you, and Linc put a stop to it. He didn't get shot because of you. He got shot because, once again, Jace is a complete piece of shit and tried to hurt not only you but Linc's brothers. You didn't ask for Jace to beat you, and you didn't ask for him to shoot Linc or come after you. You need to put the blame for this where it belongs, and that's squarely on Jace's shoulders."

"Lucy, you don't understand—"

She holds up a hand, cutting me off.

"I understand all too well, actually. Jace spent years telling you the way he acted and the things he did were your fault. That's bullshit. Jace is to blame for all of this. I'm glad Linc was there to stop him then, and the rest of the MC is here to stop him now. And I guaran-damn-tee you there isn't a single person here that holds any of this against you."

Tanya comes back over to me and wraps an arm around me as Lucy finishes her tirade.

"The doctors say he can have two people at a time in his room. I figured you would want to go with me. He's still unconscious, but they think he'll wake up soon. Thank the lord above the bullet didn't hit anything vital."

I look around the waiting area at all of Linc's brothers. I want to see him more than anything in the world, but guilt is still playing tricks with my mind.

"I'm sure his brothers want to see him and make sure he's okay. I can wait."

"And they will." Tanya's expression is understanding as she senses my trepidation. "But I promise you, the face *he'll* need to see when he wakes up is yours."

I nod because the last thing I'm going to do is argue with the woman.

"Okay."

She grasps my hand tightly, and we head to Linc's room.

The narrow hospital bed barely fits Linc's broad frame. Tanya pulled chairs next on either side of the bed, and I've been sitting on one side, with Linc's mom on the other, listening to the machines monitoring his heart rate. It's been a few hours, and there hasn't been any change. Not that I expected my presence to bring him out of wherever he is right now, but still, a girl can hope.

Tanya leaves to update the club on Linc's condition and to let one of the other brothers come in and sit with him for a bit. I feel guilty as hell that she's leaving and I'm staying, but when I offered to do it for her, she smiled and politely told me to sit my ass in the chair. Again, this is not a woman you argue with.

Jude comes in and sits in the seat Tanya vacated.

"How you holding up?" he asks, pointing to my bruised face.

"Fine. I barely feel a thing."

"I doubt that," Jude scoffs.

He's right, my face hurts like a bitch, but I'm not about to complain. I'm alive, and right now, that's good enough for me.

"Are the police going to get involved? I thought when there was a gunshot wound, the hospital had to report it to them."

"In any other situation, yes, but my brother knows a lot of people in a lot of high places." He shoots me a wry smile. "He made a couple phone calls and said we won't have to worry about it."

"Your brother's a handy guy to have around."

"That he is, though it comes with a price."

"What's the price I'm going to have to pay?"

"You? Absolutely nothing. Ozzy, on the other hand, owes him another favor."

"But it's my ex that got us in this mess."

"Doesn't matter. You're Linc's woman, which means it falls under club business."

I nod as though I understand, but honestly, what if Linc wakes up and decides it's all too much to keep me around? I would be heartbroken, sure—actually I would be devastated—but as long as he recovers, I'd find a way to live with it.

We sit in silence for a few more minutes.

"I'm going to go get Knox. I know he wants to see his brother."

I silently nod in acknowledgment.

When Jude leaves, I lay my head next to Linc's, trying not to disturb his sleeping form.

"Please open your eyes. Everyone here is waiting for you to come back."

There's no change in any of the monitors.

"Listen, if you open your eyes, I'll let you give me any nickname you want. Charlie bird? Sounds great. Charlie bug? Even better. And if you're really attached to it, you can call me Cha Cha. Anything you want. You just have to wake up."

The pressure in my bruised eye from crying is pounding through my skull, but I can't stop the tears from running over my nose and onto the pillow next to his head.

I hear his breath hitch first, then see his eyelids flutter.

"Linc?" I ask, praying to any god who will listen that this means what I think it means.

His eyes blink open, and his hazel gaze connects with my face.

"Mine," he croaks out.

"What?"

Linc clears his throat and swallows hard.

"The only thing I want to call you is mine."

Chapter Twenty-One
Unc

I hear her soft whispers before it registers what she's saying.

"If you're really attached to it, you can call me Cha Cha. Anything you want. You just have to wake up."

Charlie's voice is a broken whisper in my ear. I need to get to her, to comfort her. She needs to know I hear her and that I love her. Nothing is going to keep me from her. Attempting to open my eyes takes a few tries before the lids separate and her beautiful tear-stained face comes into view.

"Mine," I say, but it doesn't come out right. My throat is scratchy, and my voice sounds foreign to my ears. I clear my throat and try to swallow some moisture so I don't sound like a pack-a-day smoker.

"The only thing I want to call you is mine."

"Oh, thank God." Rivulets of tears run down her face, but her smile shines fucking brilliantly through the wetness.

"How do you feel?" Her voice is whisper soft as we face each other, breathing the same air, both of us beyond grateful to be alive.

"Like a bullet tore through my gut." I raise a hand and carefully brush my finger over her bruised eye. "How about you?"

"Like I got punched in the face." Charlie turns her head and kisses my palm. "I don't care about my stupid black eye," she says. "You're still with me."

"Babe, it's going to take a lot more than a bullet to keep us apart."

Her light laugh brightens her bruised face. "My tough biker."

I nod, and a painful chuckle escapes me. I'm going to have to be careful about that.

"I am yours, Charlie, and you're mine."

The softness and understanding in her gaze, as she tilts her head forward to kiss me, lets me know she gets it. We've made it to the other side, and I'm not letting her go.

"I love you," she whispers against my lips.

Charlie holds her breath for a beat before I speak.

"I love you, too."

Her lips find mine again, but she keeps the kiss gentle. If I wasn't laid up in this hospital bed, barely able to move, I would have her spread out while I made her come over and over again, telling me she loves me with every breath. I'll have to settle for her as close as I can get her.

"Come lie next to me." I want to feel all of her pressed against me. After almost losing her to that fuckwit, there's nothing I want more than to feel her body against mine.

"Linc, I don't think I'm allowed to."

"I don't give a fuck about hospital rules, sweetheart. I need you closer."

Charlie huffs and nervously looks at the door like Nurse Ratched is going to come in and yell at her for disturbing the patient.

Let them try.

She slips off her shoes and gingerly sits on the edge before turning toward me on her side.

"There, happy?"

I lean in for another kiss because there's no way in hell I'll ever get enough of her lips.

"Happiest man alive." I take a deep breath and thank whatever gods are in the universe that I have this woman next to me.

"I should find your mom and Trick. The rest of your brothers are here, too."

"Where is here, exactly?" It dawns on me I don't even know what hospital I'm at. The second I woke up and saw Charlie next to me, nothing else mattered.

"Not too far from the cabin. Jude was able to call Liam and get an ambulance to you."

The mention of Jude brings back the memory of the gunshots I heard before I passed out.

"Are he and Lucy good?"

"They're completely fine," Charlie reassures. "They were able to take cover before the guys Jace had with him got too close. When Jace took off with me, the guys went with him."

"Did she say what they looked like?" I'd really like to know who helped him.

"It wasn't the Italians," Charlie confirms, already sensing where my thoughts were headed. "She said they looked like run-of-the-mill thugs for hire. Not the same guys as Texas, but no one connected to the Italians."

"Some people would call us run-of-the-mill thugs," I muse, shooting her a wink.

Charlie leans up to kiss me. "Your anything but run of the mill," she says after she breaks the kiss.

My mom walks in the room, startling Charlie. Like a kid who's worried they've been busted, she tries to scramble off the bed.

"No honey, you stay right where you are," my mom tells her. "How are you feeling, son?"

"Just peachy," I reply dryly.

My mom doesn't blink an eye at my tone.

"I'm going to go get the nurse and let her know you're awake." She walks over and leans down, kissing my forehead. "Could you please not get shot again?"

"I'll do my best." I want to laugh at her request, but I know the movement will be as painful as it was the first time.

Giving Charlie a soft smile, she leaves the room.

"Come here," I say, tilting my head toward my woman. "I need another kiss before she gets back."

Charlie obliges before the door opens, and a nurse and the doctor enter.

They make Charlie get off the bed before looking me over, much to my dismay. Even three feet away is too far right now. The doctor tells me about my heart stopping on the way to the hospital due to severe blood loss, but once I was stabilized, they were able to perform surgery and stop the bleeding... yada yada.

"So, when can I go home?" I ask, ready to get the hell out of here.

"It's going to be at least a few days, barring any complications," he replies.

I send him a look that says, 'yeah, we'll see about that.'

My brothers are in and out of my room for the next few days, making jokes and trying to make me feel better and make the days go by faster. Charlie stays with me every night, even though she insisted I needed the rest. I told her I'd rest easier with her next to me. I feel bad about her being uncomfortable, but I'm not ready to have her away from me for more than the ten minutes it takes to get a cup of coffee or some food. I'm being a needy little bitch, but ask me if I care.

Ozzy is in the room when Charlie goes on a quick coffee run after giving me a gentle kiss on the lips.

"Where is he?" I ask my president.

Charlie told me what went down at the warehouse, and Jude told me that Jace is still alive, but I didn't want Charlie around for this conversation.

"We have him at the clubhouse. One of your brother's guys stitched him up and did some field surgery bullshit, so you'd have a chance to take care of him yourself."

"Thanks for that."

Ozzy knows what it means to me to take care of this shit myself. His dad did it for my mom, and I'll be damned if I'm not the one to send that piece of shit to hell.

"How did the Irish find them so fast?"

"Monaghan was pretty tight-lipped about it," Ozzy explains, running a hand over his stubble. "Said he had a guy and left it at that. This shit with the Irish and Italians is none of my business, and I'd like to keep it that way. It goes back way before our beef with the Italians."

The feud involving those two families is sure to bring nothing but trouble. I completely agree with my prez. Best to let sleeping dogs lie—at least for now.

Liam arranges for transport home the next day. The doctors aren't thrilled with me leaving so early, but they aren't going to convince me that lying in a hospital bed for the next few days is any better for me than lying in my own bed where my girl can sleep next to me without having to watch out for wires and all that shit.

"Of course, he got you a fucking ambulance," Ozzy says when he sees the vehicle Liam provided.

A giant man, who is definitely not an EMT, opens the back door to the rig.

"Kingston Bishop." The man introduces himself and shakes my and Ozzy's hand.

"You're the medic?" Ozzy asks.

"That was a long time ago," is his only reply.

They lay me on the stretcher in the back of the ritziest ambulance I've ever seen. Not that I've seen many, but I'm sure this is much nicer than the one that brought me here.

I sleep most of the way back to the clubhouse. Thank God since Charlie wasn't with me. The only time I don't miss her next to me is if I'm sleeping.

Knox and Ozzy say goodbye to Kingston and help me in my room, with Charlie following behind them.

"Do you need anything?" she asks when my brothers leave the room.

"Yeah." I hold out a hand to her. "For you to lie down with me."

She sits on the bed, ready to cuddle up next to me.

"Naked," I tell her before she lies down.

"Linc, you just got out of the hospital. If you think anything other than sleeping is going to happen, you're out of your damn mind."

It's cute how she thinks I won't convince her.

"Babe, I just want your skin on mine. I don't expect you to hop on and ride me."

"Okay,"—she gives me a dubious look—"but we're just going to sleep."

The couple nights I had Charlie in my bed, we slept completely naked. Granted, there was no use putting clothes back on when I was inside of her every damn time I woke up, but I loved having her warm skin touching mine without the barrier of clothing.

She takes her top and bra off, along with her shorts.

"You can leave the panties on."

The little pink lace number she's wearing barely covers anything and is sexy as hell.

When she cuddles into my side, I kiss the top of her head, and she lets out a contented sigh. Moving the arm that she isn't wrapped in, I gently graze her pink nipple with the back of my fingers. She doesn't protest, so I turn my hand over and pinch the bud, gently twisting it.

"Linc, you're breaking the rules. You're supposed to be taking it easy," Charlie whispers, looking up at me with those big blue eyes full of lust.

"I never met a rule I didn't like to break."

Charlie rolls her eyes, and I lean over for a kiss, my tongue sliding across the seam of her soft lips. She opens, and I gently explore her mouth with my tongue, plucking at her nipple as I deepen the kiss.

She pulls away, panting for breath. "We need to stop. I don't want you doing anything that could land you back in the hospital."

"I wasn't shot in the hand, baby. Let me take care of you," I say, moving my hand from her breast and dipping my fingers into her panties.

"Mmm, that feels so good," Charlie moans, any protest dying on her tongue as I circle her clit with my finger before dipping it inside her.

"You're so wet for me. God, I wish I could sink my cock into you right now."

I pump two fingers in and out of her tight channel. Her forehead is pressed against mine, her eyes squeezed shut. Using my thumb to rub her clit, it takes less than a minute before her walls begin to flutter around my fingers.

"Open your eyes, baby. I want you looking at me when you come."

Bright blue eyes meet mine, her pupils nearly blown out from arousal. She clamps down on my fingers and lets out a strangled moan as she rides her climax out on my hand.

"There is nothing hotter than watching you come apart," I say before taking her mouth in a deep, wet kiss. When her tremors subside, I remove my hand from her panties and bring it to my mouth. "Love the way you fucking taste," I say, licking the fingers that were just inside her.

"I love you, Linc."

"I love you too, baby. Let's take that nap now, yeah?"

"Mmm-hmm," she moans softly before falling asleep right where she belongs.

I wake before Charlie. The sun has set, and even though I'm sore as shit, I have a couple things to take care of.

It takes me a minute to sit up in bed and another to pull on a pair of jeans and a shirt. I slip my feet into my boots, not bothering with socks, then make my way to the main room of the clubhouse.

Jude, Knox, and Ozzy are sitting at the bar. When they see me, they rise to their feet.

"I know you think you're some kind of superhero mate, but you should really be lying next to your woman and getting some rest." Jude watches me slowly make my way to him.

"I need to take care of the trash first."

Jude looks toward Ozzy to see what he has to say while Ozzy studies me. One nod of his head is all it takes for me to know he understands this needs to happen, and I need it to happen tonight. There's no way in hell I'll be able to truly rest while that piece of shit is still breathing.

As we walk down the stairs to the large basement room with soundproof walls, my bullet wound hurts like a motherfucker. Instead of making me want to turn around and get back in bed with my woman, it spurs me on. He thought he could take me out and take my girl.

Not in this fucking life.

Ozzy opens the door, and I walk in.

Jace looks up from the chair he's tied to with a crude bandage wrapped around his middle.

"You lived," he slurs.

Even if I didn't come here tonight, there's no doubt in my mind he isn't long for this world. But I'll be damned if I let him slip into a fever dream and die in his sleep. That's way too good for this asshole.

"I guess you and that whore get to live happily ever after now."

I walk up to him like I don't have a care in the fucking world and punch him in the eye. Just like he did my girl.

"Got something else to say, fuckwad?" I ask, standing over him.

He looks at me with a cut gushing blood above his eyebrow.

"Yeah. Fuck you," he spits out.

I dig my thumb into the wound where Charlie's bullet tore through him. He lets out an ear-piercing howl of pain. Good thing for soundproof walls.

"I'm not the one who's fucked here, Jace. You came after my brothers. My woman." I dig my thumb harder. "And thought you were going to get away with it."

He doesn't apologize or beg me to spare his life. He knows this is the end.

"She will be loved and cherished like you should have done when you had her. I'll make sure she's so happy and protected every day for the rest of her life that she'll never think of you again." I pull the knife from my boot. "And you? You'll be nothing more than worm food."

Grabbing his hair, I yank his head back and slice the blade across his throat, watching with satisfaction as he chokes on his own blood. I step back and stare at his lifeless body.

"Fuck you, asshole." This isn't the first life I've taken in the name of the Black Roses, but it is the first for my girl. And just like the other times, I have no regrets.

Now that the adrenaline is wearing off, exhaustion quickly overtakes me. Knox enters the room and sees me wavering on my feet.

"I'll handle the cleanup, brother. You go back to your girl."

Normally, this would be a two-man job, but hell if I'm going to argue.

"Yeah, I think that would be a good idea."

Knox clasps me on the shoulder. "You gonna put your patch on her?"

A wide grin splits my mouth. "Hell yeah, I am."

Knox nods and turns to the body in the middle of the room without commenting further.

Jude is on the other side of the door and helps me up the stairs. Rather than going back to my room a bloody mess, we go to Jude's, and he helps me wrap my bandage in plastic and puts a folding chair in the shower for me.

"I love you like a brother, but washing your balls is too much to ask," he says when I spot the chair.

"Agreed," I reply.

After a quick shower, I change into a pair of his sweats and slowly make the trek back to my own room where Charlie is still sleeping peacefully.

The movement on the mattress when I lie down wakes her, no matter how careful I try to be.

"You okay?" she asks sleepily.

"Never better, baby."

She curls back into my side.

"I love you," she mumbles before going back to sleep.

"I love you, too," I reply, kissing her forehead before my eyes close. This time, sleep comes easy, and I follow Charlie into dreamland.

EPILOGUE
CHARLIE

"Linc," I say on a breathless laugh. "Stop. We need to get out there. You know we can't leave Lucy unattended for long."

He growls into my neck and the vibration sends chills of excitement down my spine.

"I don't give a fuck about Lucy right now. It's not our problem Jude is constantly trying to one-up her."

Three months later and Jude is still trying to find some game he can beat Lucy at, insisting it's beginner's luck every time she bests him. When she beat him at darts, I honestly thought we were about to witness a grown biker cry.

"I would just like one party that doesn't end in him storming off like a baby," I tell the man who still has his mouth attached to my neck. Oh, the wicked things he does with that mouth. Shit, the wicked things he just did with that mouth.

Linc and I found a little house not far from the club-house. Evidently, the club has a few rentals, something about diversifying their portfolio, and they had two available next door to each other.

Imagine the luck.

Lucy insisted she was perfectly happy living next door instead of us all in the same house. Apparently, she got more than an earful when we were at the cabin. It's hard to believe that was only three months ago. It feels like a lifetime.

Of course, Linc still has a room at the compound; all the brothers do. On nights when there's a party and we've had too much to drink, it's nice to only have to walk a few steps to go to bed instead of worrying about cabbing it back home. Then there're times like this when Linc can't keep his hands off me and has to sneak me away. Not that I would ever complain. Since being with Linc, I've discovered my appetite for all things carnal and delicious. The sex drive I never thought I had suddenly matches his. Looks like I just needed the right man to show me what worshiping a woman looks like.

"Okay, but Ozzy told you there was another club coming. The last thing I want is one of those guys thinking my best friend is a bunny. I don't see that going over well with her."

"Trust me babe," Linc smirks. "Jude will make damn sure every one of those guys knows not to touch her."

"He'll probably tell them she'll cut their dick off or something," I muse.

He shakes his head. "Yeah, we'll go with that."

Linc finally lets me put my clothes back on with only a few more grumbling remarks, and we make our way into the main room.

All the brothers are here, and the party is well underway. It's the same type of party Lucy and I walked into all those months ago. I don't expect these guys to change anytime soon. As long as no one touches my man, the bunnies and strippers can run around half-naked all they want.

Lucy bounds over with a beer in her hand and a wide smile on her face.

"Get this," she starts. "Jude wants to try to beat me in backgammon. Backgammon!" She lets out a loud laugh. "Apparently, he played it all the time growing up and thinks he'll wipe the floor with me." She turns to Linc. "Shouldn't he lose his patch for being an old lady or something?"

Linc chuckles and shakes his head. "Nah, we all know about his penchant for board games." He wraps an arm around my waist and pulls me close before kissing the top of my head. "I gotta go talk to Ozzy," he says, then turns to my best friend. "Behave."

Lucy holds up three fingers. "Scouts honor," she says innocently.

He doesn't buy it for a second.

"So, you guys staying all night?" Lucy asks when Linc walks away.

"Probably," I tell her. "But you don't have to."

"I don't know." She eyes the crowd of bikers. "Maybe there'll be some new blood with the crew that's coming in. I might want to have a little fun tonight."

I shake my head. Lucy isn't one for random sex, but I haven't seen her date anyone in a couple years. Now that I've been with Linc, I can't imagine going that long without sex. Then again, I'm sure not every man can do what he does, so maybe her experience is different from mine.

"Just stay out of Jude's way. I know you two get off on making each other miserable, but let's try to just have fun tonight."

"Spoilsport," she says, sticking her tongue out at me.

We hear another group of bikers walk through the door before we see them. I spot Ozzy, Knox, and Linc walking over to greet them.

"Oh, those must be the guys from Nevada."

Lucy turns around and cranes her neck to get a better look. Her head quickly swings back in my direction, and she looks pale as a ghost.

"What's wrong?" I ask, concerned with the look in her eyes.

She doesn't answer for a beat, and alarm bells are going off in my head. This isn't like my friend at all.

"Lucy," I say, grabbing her hand. "What's wrong?"

The touch shakes her out of whatever stupor she's in.

"Nothing." She takes a shaky sip of her beer. "Just thought I saw someone I recognized. Hey, let's go get another drink." Lucy turns toward the bar, and I follow her.

"Are you sure you're okay? If this is about Jude, I've told you a million times—"

"No, it has nothing to do with Jude."

"But it has to do with someone?" Why is she acting so damn cagey?

"I'm fine, Charlie." Lucy pastes on a fake-as-hell smile. "Promise." She looks over my shoulder and stills, looking like a deer in headlights.

Following her gaze, I spot a guy from the Nevada MC making his way over to us, his sights set on my friend. I don't know this guy from Adam, but there's something about him that sets me on edge.

When he reaches us, he orders a beer from the prospect behind the bar while Lucy stares at the condensation running down her bottle.

What the hell is going on?

"Ladies," the man next to me drawls. "Nice night."

I shoot him an uneasy smile while Lucy doesn't take her eyes off her beer.

"You look an awful lot like a girl I used to know back in Nevada. Ever been?" he asks my friend.

"Nope."

"Huh, that's pretty weird. A little older and you have black hair, but you're the spitting image of a girl I met back there."

Lucy shrugs without looking in his direction.

"Hey, Charlie. Let's play some pool," she says, grabbing her drink and my hand before walking toward the pool table.

"They're still looking for you, Lucinda," the biker calls.

Lucy pretends not to hear him, but the way her grip tightens around my hand tells me she heard him loud and clear.

Instead of going to the table, I drag her into the hallway that leads to the bedrooms.

"Okay, you need to tell me what the hell is going on right now. Why did he call you Lucinda?"

"I don't know. The guy is probably drunk. I look like a lot of people." Her excuse is flimsy at best.

"You know I'll never make you share anything with me you aren't comfortable with, but I think it's time you started talking. If there's something I can help with or the club—"

"It's nothing, Charlie. I've never seen that guy before in my life. Like I said, he's probably just drunk, and he's definitely mistaken."

This is pointless. I know Lucy well enough to know if she doesn't want to talk to me about something, she'll stonewall me every step of the way.

"Okay, but I'm here for you if there's anything—"

"There's not." Her eyes soften as she reaches to pull me in for a hug.

"Listen, I'm pretty tired. I'm gonna head home."

"Why don't you go lie down in our old room? You've been drinking." That's the point of keeping our rooms here, after all.

"I've only had two. Besides, I kinda want my own pillow, not those cheap ass ones on a twin bed."

We laugh at the memory of the bunny who thought if she made us uncomfortable enough, we would leave. Jokes on her. We're still here, and she's nowhere to be found.

"Okay, call me when you get home." I smile at my best friend. There's more to the story, and when she's ready, I'm certain she'll tell me. Until then, I'll just have to be patient.

"Will do," she replies and heads toward the back door, blowing me a kiss before she steps into the night air.

When I walk back into the main room, I spot Jude scowling toward the hallway I just came from. Good lord, will those two ever get along?

Linc comes and finds me back at the bar.

"Where'd Lucy go?"

"She said she was tired. I don't know, though. Something is off." I shrug as Linc grabs another beer.

"If it was something big, she would have told you, babe. Besides, I'm awfully tired myself," he says with a little pout as he bats his dark lashes.

"Really?" I quirk my brow, giving him a deadpan look.

"No," he laughs out. "Not really. But I am ready for bed."

"What about your guests?"

Linc looks back to the new group of men already enjoying what the club has to offer. And by that, I mean the strippers and lap dances.

"Let the guys entertain the boys from Nevada. I have other plans for you."

Since his plans generally include multiple orgasms, I follow him back to his room without any further protest. I'll take Linc's version of entertainment over anything going on out here.

And love every minute of it.

Thank you so much for reading Charlie and Linc's story! I absolutely loved writing them and I can't wait to share with you what I have in store for the rest of the Black Roses brothers.

If you enjoyed the book, I would be forever grateful if you left a review. Reviews are incredibly helpful to authors and it's a great way to help us spread the word about our stories.

Do you want to know what it was like for a few of my guys growing up in Shine? Join my newsletter by going to my website www.katerandallauthor.com or scan the QR code below to get the free prequel, **Rose Colored Glasses** when you sign up. It's an angsty, first-love novella featuring Ozzy and Freya. Don't worry, you'll get to know lots more about them soon.

Stalk me on my socials!

TikTok

Facebook

Instagram

Goodreads

BookBub

Scan the QR code below for a link to all my socials and to sign up for my newsletter!

xoxo

ALSO BY KATE

ACKNOWLEDGEMENTS

Where to even begin? First, thank YOU for reading my stories! Being an author has always been a dream of mine, and you make it possible every time you decide to spend your precious time reading my words.

Thank you Kiki, Megan, Colleen and Anna with the Next Step PR. You are all so amazing, and y'all have your author's backs! I thank my lucky stars that I had the courage to reach out before I even published my first book. Thank you for helping me navigate this wild ride!

Molls, my sister from another mister. Thank you for listening to my ramblings when I send you Marco Polos after I've been writing or editing all day and can barely form a coherent sentence. Your encouragement and excitement for everything I'm doing has kept me going on more than one occasion. I love you, sister.

And, of course, to the best husband in the world, Matt. Thank you for always being there when I doubt myself and for reminding me that this ride isn't over yet when I question if I can do this. You are the one that holds it together for our family when I'm in my cave getting "just a few more words" out. Love you, babe.

ABOUT KATE

Kate is a lover of all things books. It doesn't matter what genre, as long as there's a HEA, she's in. She started reading romance in high school and would hide novels in textbooks to read during class. Becoming an author was always a dream she had and finally decided to put pen to paper (or finger to keyboard) and write what she loves. She grew up in the beautiful upper peninsula of Michigan then became a West Coast girl where she lives with her amazing husband and hilarious son. She would love to hear from readers so check out all her socials and sign up for her newsletter so she can keep you up to date on her books and whatever other ramblings come to mind.

Made in the USA
Columbia, SC
08 March 2024

32281495R00186